EMERALD SECRET

EMERALD SECRET

SUSAN MOORE

nosy crow

First published in the UK in 2017 by Nosy Crow Ltd
The Crow's Nest, 10a Lant Street
London, SE1 1QR, UK

Nosy Crow and associated logos are trademarks and/or registered
trademarks of Nosy Crow Ltd

Text © Susan Moore, 2017
Cover © Alessandro "Talexi" Taini, 2017

Printed and bound in the UK by Clays Ltd, St Ives Plc
Typeset by Tiger Media

Papers used by Nosy Crow are made from wood grown in
sustainable forests.

ISBN: 978 0 85763 8267

www.nosycrow.com

For Mum and Dad

FUTURE TECH AND OTHER COOL STUFF

BEETLEBOT: A robotic, flying cockroach with flex-diamond-coated shell and retractable wings. Water-resistant, fully-loaded with nanotech eye cameras. Available shades: Burnt Chocolate, Soggy Beetroot. Designed and manufactured by Spysecta.

FASTPAD: A flexible, tough, wafer-thin tablet computer, which can be rolled up. Invented by UK-based technology company Fenomenell.

GROOVERIDER: A low-slung, hydrogen-powered sports car with a distinctive grooved bonnet. Designed and manufactured by Choprider, Shanghai.

OCTOZEB GOGGLES: Diamond-def, virtual-reality goggles designed and made by SPIN, Hong Kong.

OVERRIDER: A super-sized, six-wheeled all-terrain truck. Originally developed for the Chinese army by Choprider, Shanghai.

POPKO JUICE: A range of juice smoothies served in striped layers containing a secret Popko ingredient.

ROCKETBOAT: A hydrogen-powered, cigar-shaped speedboat, capable of rapid acceleration and speeds of up to 200mph.

SLIDER: A skateboard-shaped, electrically powered hover board with pop-up handlebars. The Slider was invented by Beijing Bikes' top engineer, Liu Lee, using the same principles of motion as the classic hovercraft from the twentieth century.

SMART T-SHIRT: An e-textile T-shirt containing soft, flexible screens on the front and back for display of movie clips, photos or text.

SPIN: The world's largest virtual-reality games company. Designers and builders of three bestselling games — "Empire of the Shadow", "Wand of Truth" and "Lavanter". Founded by Max and Catherine Walker. Headquarters — Hong Kong.

WARZWORLD: Virtual-reality games company with fully immersive war worlds ranging from Aztec kingdoms to Alien planets. Players must be certified 18 to play. Founded by Baroness Ivy Shiversand. Headquarters — London.

Chapter One
LONDON

The north wind was whistling through the rigging, batting the wolf's head flag against the top of the mast. Fingers of pale sunlight crept across the polished wooden deck, up and over an orange hammock that was swinging from the front boom of the boat.

Nat lay dozing inside, cocooned in her sleeping bag, dreaming she was still in Hong Kong.

"AHOY there!"

A booming voice came blasting through the thin fabric.

"Yeouch!" A red-hot poker of pain shot up her arm.

Her eyes snapped open to find a pair of amber eyes flashing through a fug of smoke.

"*Sorry,*" said Fizz. "*I didn't mean to burn you. I set my intruder alert to 'high' last night when we entered the river.*"

Nat pulled down the top of the bag and a gush of icy air greeted her. She squinted in the early morning dawn. Her arm really hurt, with a red whip-like mark forming across the skin.

"*Zoinks*, Fizz. I'm not an intruder!"

Her dragon robot lowered his snout and swept a green-scaled wing across his chest, taking a deep bow.

"*Forgive me, my lady. I'd perchance set myself to be too sensitive in my effort to valiantly protect thee,*" he said, his voice low, in an accent that was a million miles away from his normal, digital one.

"Why on earth are you talking like that?"

He raised his head.

"*An ad came up last night in my BotBox for a 'free British accent and mannerisms download' for foreign robots. 'Give yourself a classy edge and act like a local in London.'*"

Nat sighed.

"*You don't like it?*" asked Fizz.

"Just stay the ku dragon that you are. There are enough crazy changes happening right now."

"*I just want to fit in.*"

She did too, more than anything – to blend in, not to be noticed.

"AHOY!" The booming voice came again.

Nat clapped her hands over her ears. *Rats' tails…* She swung her legs over the side of the hammock and jumped down on to the rain-slicked deck. Her teeth chattered as the damp cut through the old purple kung fu suit that she'd repurposed into pyjamas.

"*Voice overboard, starboard thirty-two degrees,*" said Fizz, still in the hammock.

"Would have been *ku* if you'd detected that before you burned my arm," Nat muttered, stepping over a coiled mooring rope to reach the side of the boat.

Leaning over the brass rail she found a navy-blue Rocketboat cruising alongside on the murky brown river below. The word "POLICE" was stamped in bold scarlet letters on the hull.

On deck stood a policeman wearing a black top hat and a long navy frock coat with shiny gold buttons, with a bushy beard down to his waist.

"How many crew are you, young lady?" he bellowed through an old-fashioned hand-held megaphone.

"Three and one robot!" she shouted back, wondering why he needed to know.

The policeman frowned. "You should have more crew to handle such an ancient vessel."

"This is an 'oversize replica of a Ming Dynasty treasure ship'!" she shouted, using Jamuka's words. "It's only fourteen years old and runs on a MaxEdge computer. It can sail without crew."

The policeman let out a low whistle and turned to

speak to his colleague at the helm.

Nat yawned and looked over at the riverbank, which was lined with rows of brick warehouse buildings and glass office blocks. It was all much lower than Hong Kong's spiky skyline.

"Request to speak with your captain immediately!" said the policeman, still holding his megaphone.

She stepped away from the rail and turned to Fizz.

"Go and find Jamuka, quick."

"*Aye, aye,*" he said.

She watched the little robot take off, shooting through the air like a green arrow. She still wasn't used to the idea that he could fly.

The air tasted different from when she'd gone to sleep. They'd been crossing the North Sea then. Now they were on the Thames and it wasn't just salty, but musty too, reminding her of Ken's kung fu studio. It'd be a long time before she was back there again.

Burnt coffee wafted up from the open hatch that Fizz had passed through. Jamuka must already be up. She guessed he was probably in the kitchen, watching the horses from Hong Kong on his FastPad. His horse, Dragon Khan, would be getting warmed up for his race.

She shivered. Maybe she should go and grab her

Slider jacket. She reached the hatch just as Jamuka stepped out on to deck, fully dressed in his customary long, midnight-blue mandarin suit with silver buttons. His grey hair was plaited into a ponytail, tied off with a black ribbon, and his eyes were shielded by round mirrored sunglasses. In one hand he held a steaming cup. In the other he was carrying the bamboo cage containing his prized green and white songbird, Gobi.

Fizz had perched on top of her cage. Gobi had her head back, looking up at him, singing in her high, chirping voice. She'd only started doing that since Fizz had his flying upgrade.

The smell of burnt coffee was so strong now it made her stomach churn.

"I thought you'd given up Vietnamese weasel coffee?" she said, wrinkling her nose.

"I need it to draw strength, Bao Bao. Dragon Khan went lame in the race. Now, I hear we have visitors."

She pointed over at the police boat. Jamuka handed her Gobi's cage and strode across to talk to the policemen.

If Dragon Khan was lame Jamuka was going to be on calls to his vet and trainer for hours. Maybe they'd have to fly back to Hong Kong to check on him, then she wouldn't have to go to this silly school in London.

She could stay with her best friend, Wen.

The boat's engines cut. Their low hum was replaced with the droning sound of city traffic.

"We're off autopilot," Jamuka called. "The river police want a manual entry. Dock rules, Bao Bao."

Nat gulped. "Manual?"

She had a sudden flashback to the last time they'd manually docked the boat, and the brass band running out of their path as Jamuka reversed straight into the pier at the Harbour Club regatta using full throttle reverse by mistake.

Chapter Two
BEETLEBOT

The beetlebot's antennae twitched, waking it up from sleep mode. The target destination was in range. It raised its flex-diamond-coated brown shell to release its wings, and took off from where it had been camped out all night on the riverbank.

A strong headwind was coming up the Thames, making progress slow flying over the water.

Up ahead the target was looming large through the beetlebot's nanotech eye camera. It cross-checked the boat with the stored image it had been given. Direct match. *Junko* boat confirmed.

Its antennae twitched again. "*Warning – police presence detected*" came flashing through its databanks. Since it didn't have a river robot licence it switched to "covert-ops" mode.

The *Junko*'s deck was now visible. The beetlebot scanned and locked on to the tall girl with red hair, dressed in a purple kung fu suit. It image-checked again. Direct match; Natalie Walker confirmed.

A red flashing light popped up to the left of its camera. It zoomed in to detect a policeman climbing a ladder up the side of the *Junko*. Time calculation showed forty seconds to him reaching the deck where the girl was standing.

The beetlebot accelerated wing speed to max. It flew as straight as an arrow towards the girl, programmed to complete its mission in the quickest time possible.

Ten seconds from contact. It was about to open up its underbelly to get the delivery ready, when "*ZING!*", an electric-blue laser light shot straight through its body, immobilising its central processor. The *Junko*'s security system sent a shockwave bouncing it away with such force that it was propelled through the air, "*PLOP!*", into the Thames below.

Chapter Three
AN INVITATION

A shadow fell over Nat. She looked up to find the policeman with the megaphone. He removed his top hat and made a low bow.

"Permission to come aboard, young lady, to help bring you in safely…"

He spotted Fizz and his mouth dropped open. "What kind of creature are you?"

Fizz ruffled his wings. *"I am a unique, custom-made dragon robot."*

He snorted a thin stream of orange flames out of his snout.

"We could do with a dragon like you in the Metropolitan Police Force to help fight crime."

"All hands on deck!" shouted Jamuka from the helm.

Ah Ping's head popped up from the fore hatch, before she darted across the deck. Her navy jacket and shorts were heavily creased, and her black hair was messily knotted back. She yawned, then gave Nat and the policeman a curt nod before rushing towards the stern to get her orders from Jamuka.

Nat looked over the bow. They were coming around a bend. The rumbling of a city at work carried in on the wind.

"What's that?" she said, pointing at two ancient, square towers looming up out of the river ahead.

"Tower Bridge," said the policeman.

"*Zoinks*, looks like a castle!"

"*Home sweet home*," said Fizz.

Nat sucked in the cool air through her teeth. "Hey, wait a minute, Fizz..."

"Time to prepare," said the policeman. "Fine dragon, I need you to scan for river traffic. It's a busy time and with this boat we need to make sure we are clear."

Fizz's eyes glowed purple. He raised a talon, disconnected his Spiderwire charge-up and flew off to perch high on the foremast.

"Prepare for the lock!" shouted Jamuka.

Nat's heart began to thud. They were nearly at St Katharine Docks. Her journey from Hong Kong was coming to an end.

The boat started to turn as a siren sounded from the right bank. She looked across the water to where a large moss-covered gate was swinging open, revealing a narrow channel.

"Not in a trillion years are we ever going to fit through that!"

"By my calculation we can fit in the lock. Though it will be fingers in glove," called Fizz from the mast.

"Hand in glove. *Ai yah!* I hope you're right."

Nat gritted her teeth. Crossing the vast oceans, tossed over waves and turned in the swell, the *Junko* had seemed small and fragile, but here, hemmed in by land, it felt like a gigantic, floating island.

"To your ropes!" shouted Jamuka.

She leapt into action. Jamuka started to nose the *Junko* into the lock. Murky brown water cascaded through an ancient black lock gate at the other end. It was spilling in from so high up it could sink them. Nat was sure they were going to end up at the bottom of the Thames.

"Slow down!" bellowed Fizz, smoke pouring out of his snout.

"Reverse thrust!" ordered the policeman.

Jamuka pushed the *Junko*'s engines into reverse. A loud roar erupted as the propellers churned the water into a bubbling cauldron of brown froth, turning the lock into a giant jacuzzi.

Quick as lightning Nat unclipped the life-raft bag from the mast, sprinted to the front rail where water was now gushing down on to the deck, hooked the bag on to a rope and pulled the emergency inflation cord.

WOOF! The yellow life raft blew up in front of the prow. The prow nosed into it, pushing the doughnut-shaped raft up against the lock gate. The cover stretched so tight she thought it would burst. But just as she covered her ears, ready for a deafening *POP!* the boat bounced back.

"Cut engines!" shouted the policeman.

The roar vanished. The *Junko* stilled, holding steady. Behind them the gate to the Thames began to close, sealing them in.

"Good thinking, young lady," said the policeman, tipping his hat at her.

She wiped the mucky river water off her face. Her old kung fu suit was soaked through.

A torrent of water started to gush through an upper channel.

"*Lock filling. Haul in the raft,*" said Fizz, swooping down to land on her shoulder.

She unhooked the raft from the rope as Ah Ping came sprinting across the deck.

"I help," she said.

The policeman stepped forward. Between the three of them they dragged the wet raft up over the prow.

A large group of onlookers were now gathered on the quay below, filming their progress.

"*Delivery for Miss Walker!*" someone shouted in a tinny-sounding voice.

Nat frowned. How could anyone know her here, on the other side of the world?

"*There's a beetlebot at the gate,*" said Fizz. "*It's holding an envelope, one of those old-fashioned ones made out of trees. It's addressed to you.*"

She looked over to where Fizz's snout was pointing. A shiny, robotic brown beetle with long antennae had its beady black eyes fixed upon her. It was dripping with water, holding a cream envelope up between its hairy legs.

"Yeuch, it's a giant termite!"

"*Correction. It's a giant cockroach.*"

"Even worse."

"*I agree. At least you don't have to be cordial to it,*" said Fizz, flying down to the quayside.

He returned swiftly, the envelope grasped in his talons. She took it from him. On the front someone had written *Natalie Walker* in fancy, black-inked handwriting. Flipping it over she found the initials "I.S." stamped into the paper in gold foil.

She slid her hand under the flap and opened it. Inside lay a thick, cream invitation.

Baroness Ivy Shiversand
Requests the Pleasure of
NATALIE WALKER
to afternoon tea
On April 14th
at 4pm
Shiversand Manor, London
No need to R.S.V.P. Saskia will escort you from
Boxbury School

"But that's tomorrow. My first day of school!" she groaned.

She'd no idea who Baroness Ivy Shiversand was, or Saskia, but she had no interest in going there for tea. London life sucked already and they'd only just arrived.

Chapter Four
IVY

Ivy Shiversand tried to frown, but the Cementer paint had given her frozen-in-time skin, leaving her moon-shaped face wrinkle-free forever. She had been standing for two hours, motionless, one hand holding a golden spear, the other a jewelled shield. The armour suit she was wearing felt like a lead weight, even though it was woven out of light-as-a-feather silver Spiderwire.

It was her crown that was annoying her more than anything though. Even with the extra padding it was cutting in above her left ear in a most uncomfortable way. She was cross with herself for insisting that she pose for the portrait wearing the genuine solid-gold one studded with rubies. A fake crown would have done the job, but then again, maybe not, since Alton Hanbury was painting her.

She shifted her gaze from the window to where Alton was sitting at his easel in the middle of her office, or War Room, as she liked to call it. With his mad mop of brown and grey flecked hair, long bushy beard and crumpled clothes, he looked like he hadn't slept for days. He was leaning in towards the canvas, brow concertinaed in concentration. He moved his gaze back to the palette in his hand and raised his brush.

"You moved! The light on your FACE has changed!" he roared, looking up.

Ivy jumped. No one ever dared shout at her. His palette came whizzing across the room like a Frisbee, paint flying everywhere. She ducked just in time. It flew over her crown, hitting the wood-panelled wall behind her with a loud BANG!

Alton Hanbury wrenched the canvas from the easel and stomped off, his biker boots thudding across the polished floorboards.

"STOP!" shouted Ivy. "I command you!"

But the door slammed and the artist was gone. Ivy let her shield and spear clatter to the floor, then waddled across the room to put her crown back on the shelf above her throne.

"Mater, what did you do to Alton?" said her daughter, marching into the room.

Ivy turned to find Saskia dressed in a camouflage-patterned, full-length corseted dress, with her robot poodle, Poxo, in matching coat and top hat. She'd ringleted her chestnut hair and piled it up high on her head.

"Another new dress?" said Ivy, ignoring her question.

"It was delivered this morning."

Saskia's hand flew to her mouth as she spotted the paint-spattered wall from across the room.

"I moved," said Ivy, sitting down on her gold throne. "He'll have to come back again when he's calmed down."

"Has he nearly finished it?"

"I have no idea. He won't let me see it until it's complete. That was part of the very expensive deal. If he wasn't the best artist in England I'd have him chained to my throne until the work was done. As it is, I shall have to be patient."

She drummed her sweaty fingers on the arm of her throne. Patience was not her strong suit.

A drumroll came blasting out of the speakers set into the side of her throne. She looked across at the door. Beetlebot Beta, his cockroach antennae flashing bright red, came scuttling in at top speed.

"*The auction is about to start, Baroness,*" he announced in his squeaky voice.

"Ah good, a welcome distraction for us. I do like a good sale. Screen it."

Automatic blinds whooshed down to cover the floor-to-ceiling windows, blocking out the stunning views over London. The fake, flickering candles on the chandelier dimmed. On the wall opposite, an oil painting of a medieval castle slid to one side to reveal a gigantic FlexScreen. A live feed from the auction room at Bateleys appeared. Customers were gathered, ready to place bids on the sale items.

It was a busy day there. Every seat in the house was taken.

"Get my bidder, Beta."

A woman's reedy voice came over the Veltron speakers. "Baroness Shiversand, how nice to speak with you. Your timing is perfect. The lot you requested is next up for auction."

Ivy glanced back at Saskia, who was busy checking her messages on her poodle's earflap, which had flipped into a mini-screen.

"Watch and learn, please, Saskia."

The auctioneer waved his hand towards a Bateleys assistant who was standing to one side of the stage. She was holding up a long, silk-lined wooden box for the audience to view. Inside lay a sword.

EMERALD SECRET

Ivy's heartbeat quickened and her mouth went dry. This might be it.

"Zoom in on the sword," she ordered.

Beta zoomed. A double-edged straight sword appeared full-screen. A layer of rust covered its surface. The handle was curved to fit a hand.

"Lot two hundred and eighty-three. A fine fighting sword, estimated to be three thousand two hundred years old, discovered in Laozhoulin River in China. Let's start the bidding at fifty thousand pounds, shall we?"

As an initial flurry of bids got underway, Ivy let out a sigh.

"One million," came a nasal-sounding voice over the loudspeakers.

It was followed by a collective gasp from the audience. Ivy gripped the arms of her throne.

"Whose bid was that?"

Beta's beetle eyes darted from side to side as he scanned the room from Bateleys' live camera feed.

"It's another phone-in," said Ivy's bidder.

"One million. Do I hear more?" said the auctioneer.

Ivy snorted. "Bidder, get my bids out; put whoever it is under pressure."

"Yes, madam."

The auctioneer's hand flew up to the nanodot earphone stuck to his right ear.

"I have another phone-in bid for two million. Do I hear two million five hundred thousand?"

The auction room went quiet. The auctioneer cupped his hand over his ear, his eyes closed in concentration.

"Good. Two million five hun— I have another bid for four million," he announced.

The audience gasped. Ivy tried to force her Cementered lips into a painful smile.

"Good. Keep the pressure on the bidding."

The bids rocketed up.

"Six million," said the auctioneer.

Ivy felt sweat bead up at her neck and start to trickle down her back. Who would dare to outbid her?

"Madam, we are nearly at your upper limit of seven million," said the bidder.

"Seven million, five hundred. Do I hear a bid for eight million?" said the auctioneer.

"Madam?" said the bidder.

The image of the rusty sword played in her mind's eye. It could be the one … but if it wasn't, then it would be a very costly mistake.

"Madam?"

"Eight. Make it eight," she croaked.

Her throat was dry, parched. She had to spit out the words.

"Eight million pounds, ladies and gentlemen. Do I hear eight million, five?" said the auctioneer.

Silence fell across the auction room.

"Going, going, gone!"

The auctioneer banged the gavel down hard on the desk. Applause broke out across the auction room. Ivy clasped her hands together.

"Mater! That is an enormous sum," said Saskia.

Ivy swung round.

"As you well know, Saskia, I always get what I want, no matter the cost."

"But what if it isn't the right sword?"

Ivy gritted her teeth. "Then we will continue the search. Besides, the Walker girl is on her way. If we can't find it, I know she will."

Beetlebot Alpha came through the door and scuttled up her armoured leg before leaping into her lap. He looked up at her with his beady eyes.

"*Mission complete*," he said. "*The invitation is delivered to Natalie Walker.*"

Ivy would have smiled if she could have moved the muscles under her Cementered face. She must get Alton back fast. Now that the sword that would "transform her into the true warrior queen of everlasting youth and power" seemed within her grasp, she needed the portrait to be finished quickly. Then she'd have the portrait of "before", and she'd ask Alton to paint her again "after". She purred inside at how magnificent, powerful and beautiful she would be then. A total makeover.

"Good work, Alpha. Two irons in the fire. Another sword to test, and the Walker girl in our sights."

Chapter Five
BOXBURY

Nat was standing in her cabin dressed in the Boxbury School uniform that had been waiting for her at their mooring in St Katharine Docks. It was dark outside. She yawned. It had been a very long day.

"Call Wen," she said, wriggling in the corseted brown jacket. It was so tight she could barely draw breath.

Looking down, she scowled at the crested Boxbury badge with a pig's head in its centre, hand-stitched to the top pocket. The high, frilled-collar blouse felt stiff and scratchy. Worst of all was the full-length brown skirt like a heavy blanket.

Fizz clacked his talons on the metal shelf above the mirror. He spread his wings. Their emerald-green scales locked together to form a small, hi-def diamond-coated screen. Their colour faded as Wen's round face appeared, filling the screen.

"*Ai yah!* They cannot seriously expect you to wear that uniform!" cried Wen. "You look like Mary

Poppins. You won't even be able to hop on your Slider!"

Nat hobbled across to her bunk and picked up a lady's brown top hat with fishnet veil.

"This is what we're meant to wear when we're out in the city," she said, putting it on.

Wen's hands flew to her mouth. She screamed. Nat wanted to cry. She ripped the hat off and hurled it back on to the bunk before flopping down into a brown heap on the sheepskin rug.

"I wish you were here. It wouldn't be so bad if we were both going. I'm dreading tomorrow," she said.

"Ahem... I will be accompanying you, and I will be wearing the uniform too," said Fizz.

Nat picked up a small grey box. She lifted the lid and held it up to the screen. Inside lay a tiny brown and gold striped tie.

"It's hardly the same."

Wen's face loomed larger on screen as she leaned into the camera to take a good look inside the box.

"Ding! A uniform tie for a robot. Fizz will be rocking his look, but, Jade babe, you're going to be so way last century!"

Nat unhooked her jacket and pulled it off. She tugged her blouse out of the tight waistline of the skirt. She'd not worn this many layers since she was in snowy Mongolia.

"London is weird. Jamuka's the only happy one because he fits right in."

Wen snapped her fingers. Instantly "Robot Dreams", their favourite tune, started blasting through Fizz's Veltron speakers. Nat felt herself relax.

On the screen she watched Wen walk off camera, leaving a view of her very messy bedroom. It looked like she'd emptied her wardrobe on to the bed. Designer dresses, skirts, tops and jeans lay in tangled heaps. Some still had the price tags attached. The floor was littered with shoes, boots and cans of hair paint.

Wen reappeared, blocking the mess. She was holding up a blue T-shirt with the words *"Jade Babe Rocks London"* in big silver letters across the front.

"Surprise! Made this for you with my new 3D printer last night, but figured you needed to see it right now, before I send it."

Nat smiled. It made her homesick for Hong Kong.

"Thanks. Not sure I'm up to rockin' it though."

Wen pointed her finger at the screen. "You will be."

Nat caught sight of the invitation that she'd tossed on the floor earlier. She leaned across the rug, picked it up and held it up to Fizz's screen.

Wen let out a low whistle.

"Tea with a baroness? You must be important."

There was a knock on the cabin door.

"Bao Bao, into bed, please. It's late and you have school in the morning," called Jamuka.

She grimaced at Wen. "I'd better go. I'll send news tomorrow."

Later that night a cold gust of wind blew across the deck, rattling the rigging overhead and waking Nat up. She wriggled further down inside her sleeping bag. Maybe her move up on deck wasn't the best plan now they were moored.

Fizz lay curled up next to her on the pillow, in sleep mode. He was already wearing his school tie, to save time in the morning. He was excited; she was full of dread. This whole new life filled with terrible things was all because her parents had put one line in their wills: *When our dearest daughter turns thirteen, she must go to Boxbury School in London for two full school years.*

The latch on the main hatch clicked open. Glancing across the deck she saw Jamuka appear in his thick Mongolian coat and fur hat. He headed over holding a steaming mug.

"You'll catch cold out here, Bao Bao."

A crackling sound came from the mug. He handed it to her. She smiled.

"Thanks."

"Hot chocolate with popping candy."

"It's nowhere near as cold as it was when we were in Mongolia, but I feel colder," she said, as the milky warmth flowed into her hands.

Jamuka stretched his arms above his head.

"It is a different kind of cold. The damp is rising. It seeps into us, making our bones ache."

She took a sip of the hot chocolate. The candy popped, darting like a firecracker across her tongue.

"I am concerned that we have already become a spectacle here at the dock. The crowds that gathered at the *Junko*'s docking give me cause for concern about our safety and privacy. We might need to consider moving on to land."

Nat nearly dropped her mug.

"Forget it! No way am I leaving the *Junko*!"

Her guardian raised an eyebrow. "Resist the impulse to overreact."

"I know I don't like the tourists staring, but this is my home..."

The thought of moving on to dry land was

unthinkable. She could count on one hand the nights in her life not spent on the water; she couldn't sleep without the rocking motion of the waves.

"*We could cloak the* Junko, *creating a stealth field. It is a tactic used in the classic movies of* Star Wars," said Fizz.

Jamuka looked up at the masts then back down at the deck. He pursed his lips in calculation.

"Cloaking is a good plan, Fizz," he said. "We could lower the flag, and nanomesh the hull and masts with a grey-toned film. That way light will still come in through the portholes. Then it is only our shape which is showing, and not all the fancy paintwork and carvings."

Nat patted Fizz on the head. She would buy him any weird English accent modifier that he wanted!

"Jamuka, do I really have to go to this tea tomorrow?"

"Since Baroness Shiversand is on the board of governors at Boxbury School, it is wise and prudent to go. I am sure she will be most gracious and welcoming."

Chapter Six
TIGER-STYLE

Nat crouched down into horse stance, her legs wide, bare feet firmly planted on the sparring mat. She opened her arms and tried to focus, channelling energy into her fingers, clenching them into a claw shape.

Opposite stood Jamuka, eyes fixed upon her, waiting for her next move. They were in the *Junko*'s white-walled dojo, where even on the highest seas he'd insisted she did her daily kung fu practice. It was only six o'clock but the morning sun was already throwing a pale light against the newly mesh-screened portholes.

A lazy fly that must have hitched a ride from a warmer climate buzzed across her vision, coming to land on the sleeve of her red kung fu jacket. Irritated, she flicked it off.

"Do not be affected by another life passing by. Retain your unwavering focus," said Jamuka.

She threw up her arms and flopped down on to the mat.

"*Zoinks!* I can't do unwavering focus this morning. Do I really have to go to this new school?"

The sick feeling again. Her whole school life to date had been at Weiwood School back in Hong Kong, up on The Peak. She couldn't say it was her favourite place on the planet but right now she'd happily agree to go there seven days a week if it meant she didn't have to go to Boxbury.

Jamuka folded his arms across his chest.

"Bao Bao, it is your parents' wish that you go."

"*Was.* I bet they hadn't really thought it out, sending their only child away to school on the other side of the world. It's child cruelty. Please, please can we go home? I'll do anything."

Jamuka put his arm on her shoulder. "You already know my answer. I am duty-bound to follow your parents' wishes. Now, channel that negative energy into a positive, final few minutes of Tiger Style."

Even from the grave her parents ran her life.

"Ready?"

Outside the sun disappeared behind a cloud, casting the dojo into shadow. Nat blinked. Jamuka was back in place, awaiting her move. She wanted to run her own life, couldn't wait to decide where and what she did. Frustration bubbled up. She squatted into horse stance again and opened her arms out. This time she felt a familiar surge of energy pulsing through her. She flexed her fingers back into claws.

She was poised. In a flash her right hand shot out at Jamuka in a tiger claw strike. His arm shot out, blocking her. Not to be outdone she swatted with her left hand, but he dodged backwards. She missed his arm but caught the hanging silk sleeve of his jacket, her nails tearing through the fabric.

He spun round, ripping away from her. She had to react fast as he raised his right leg. His bare foot cut through the air in a high leg kick. She ducked and it narrowly missed her ear.

Gone were the days when Jamuka showed her any mercy, teaching her as his novice. Since their adventures in Mongolia, he sparred with her as an equal.

The door to the dojo slid open. Ah Ping appeared, dressed in a blue shirt and long shorts.

"The dock security guard called. Your Grooverider has arrived."

"Thank you. I will come up," said Jamuka. He bowed to Nat. "Good work, Bao Bao. It is time to get ready."

Back in her cabin Nat found Fizz perched on the

edge of her breakfast bowl. Only his green scaly tail was visible as he leaned over, dipping his snout.

"What are you doing?" she said, crossing the fur rug to her desk.

His head popped up. The tip of his snout was covered in a white cream.

"*I am tasting your breakfast. Ah Ping dropped it off and said the yoghurt here tastes like a Kowloon dog's dinner. My Sensomatic receptors tell me that it is five point two per cent more acidic, and I am detecting a four point seven per cent increase in lactobacilli to what you normally ingest.*"

Nat wrinkled her nose. "Yuck!"

"*Please try it and let me know what you think,*" he added.

She used her jacket sleeve to wipe his snout clean.

"After that description I'm not sure I want to."

"*But you have different taste to Ah Ping, and your ancestors ate this diet, so there is a fifty three per cent possibility that you will like it.*"

She dipped her little finger into the bowl and held it up to her nose. The yoghurt smelt rich and earthy. Putting it to her lips her eyes widened in surprise.

"*Zoinks!* Beats that fermented sheep milk I drank in Mongolia. It's good."

EMERALD SECRET

She picked a spoon up off the tray and ate a couple of mouthfuls.

"Five minutes!" shouted Ah Ping from down the corridor.

She stared at the photo of her dad that she'd stuck to the wall at the side of her bunk. He was standing under the Boxbury School front porch in a white shirt, his tie whipping sideways in a gale. Autumn leaves swirled up around his brown trousers. He was frowning into the camera. Now it was her turn.

Chapter Seven
MR LIMPET

Light rain was beginning to drizzle down the glass. Nat looked out of the Grooverider window at men on penny-farthing bikes and ladies in crinoline dresses that looked like lampshades.

"This is torture," she said, shifting uncomfortably in her uniform.

Jamuka looked up from his FastPad where he was checking the vet's report on Dragon Khan. He peered at the glowing blue dashboard over his half-moon spectacles.

"After this next set of traffic lights we should move more swiftly."

The Grooverider started to glide forward again. A few minutes later they turned into a handsome square and came to a smooth stop.

"*You have arrived at your destination. Please alight here,*" announced the onboard computer.

The Plastobend doors automatically slid upwards, curving into their slots on the roof. A cool blast of air invaded the cocooned warmth of the Grooverider. Nat's stomach did a somersault.

"Ready, Bao Bao?" said Jamuka, slipping his FastPad into his suit pocket.

She frowned and put the hat on her head. A girl in the same uniform walked by with her veil covering her face. Nat pulled hers down too.

"No. I will never be ready for this. But we might as well get it over and done with."

She hitched up her skirt and stepped out on to the pavement, across from a small park surrounded by high, black, wrought-iron railings. Tall trees swayed in the breeze, casting long shadows over a lawn criss-crossed with paths. In the centre stood a black and white building.

"*Does Gobi have to come in too?*" whispered Fizz as he landed on her shoulder.

"She's no—"

Nat didn't finish the sentence because Jamuka appeared at her side, holding the cage with Gobi chirping inside. The Grooverider started to glide off into the traffic to park.

"*Zoinks!* I thought she was only coming for the ride. We look like a circus. You can't bring her in. That's too embarrassing!" she said, panic making her voice squeaky.

Jamuka set off up the steps towards the tall wooden entrance doors of Boxbury.

"She will bring us good luck," he said.

Nat rolled her eyes and hurried after him.

Jamuka reached the school doors. Several pupils came rushing past them with their robots perched on their shoulders. Nat spotted a couple of rabbits and several dogs. A security guard appeared in a navy-blue uniform, "Boxbury School" embroidered in white letters on his top pocket. He looked sternly from Gobi to Jamuka to Nat to Fizz.

"Jamuka Borjigin and Natalie Walker to meet with Mr Limpet," said Jamuka.

The guard's expression changed. A big smile spread across his face. He stepped backwards, welcoming them inside with a sweep of the hand.

"It is a pleasure to meet you both. Mr Limpet has asked that I personally escort you to his office. Please follow me."

His voice echoed around the large, marble entrance hall. The walls were lined with wooden boards covered in dates and names in gold lettering. Nat peered closely at one to see that it was a listing of the "Boxbury Girls' First Hockey Team" from a couple of decades ago. Hockey? She didn't have a clue how to play it.

They walked past a wide, oak staircase and turned down a long corridor lined with official school photographs through the years. The smell of school dinners, floor polish and musty cupboards wafted around them.

Kids in uniform were walking along, clustered in groups, chattering loudly. They paused to check out Nat and Jamuka as they walked by. A few of them spotted Fizz on her shoulder and gave him a second look, pointing at him. A couple laughed when they saw Gobi chirping in her cage.

The security guard stopped at an oak door with the word "HEADMASTER" emblazoned across it in gold lettering. He knocked and walked inside, leaving the door open for them to follow.

"Mr Borjigin, guardian of Miss Natalie Walker, what a pleasure to make your acquaintance!"

Nat peeked out from behind Jamuka. A thin, stooped man with slicked-back silver hair stood up from behind a large, leather-topped desk. He was dressed in a black frock coat and grey pinstripe trousers. Underneath his bushy eyebrows his eyes bulged out, fizzing with an intensity that made Nat think of a frog that had drunk too much Popko juice. His brown and gold striped tie was held in place by an enormous ruby tiepin. Next to him stood a gold micro-pig robot.

"Jamuka, please," said Jamuka, shaking the headmaster's hand.

"Then I insist you call me Alger." He moved his attention to Gobi's cage.

"I do believe this is a yellow-throated laughing-thrush, Latin name *Garrulax galbanus.*"

Gobi started to chirp. "You are indeed correct," said Jamuka.

The pig oinked and trotted over to Nat. It was looking up intently at Fizz with its red eyes.

"Natalie Walker, you are the embodiment of both your dear parents. You have your father's eyes, your mother's shape of face, and her hair. I have been eager to make your acquaintance."

He stepped over, took her hand and bowed his head. The pig didn't take its eyes off Fizz. Fizz was staring right back at it. He didn't like other robots staring at him. Out of the corner of her eye she saw his eyes change from glowing green to orange.

"It's nice to meet you," she said.

Alger looked across at Fizz. Reaching into his top

pocket he pulled out an old-fashioned gold-framed monocle, fixed it to his right eye and peered in closely.

A thin wisp of smoke spooled out of Fizz's snout. Nat held her breath.

"You are magnificent," said Alger.

"My dad made him for me when I was born," said Nat.

Fizz's eyes changed back to green. Panic over.

"Quite magnificent," he continued. "A masterpiece."

Fizz ruffled his scales like a preening peacock.

"*Thank you, sir,*" said Fizz.

Sir? Nat raised her eyebrows. That was a first.

Alger removed the monocle and stood back, shaking his head.

"Max Walker was a challenging boy, always asking so many questions in my ancient history class. So much energy in him, I wondered how he'd ever channel it all."

He looked Nat in the eye.

"And now we know! He created SPIN and made it into the biggest computer-games company in the world, becoming mega-rich in the process. What an achievement!"

There was a knock on the door.

"Enter!" called Alger.

A tall girl with dark hair, who looked a couple of years older than Nat, walked in with a black poodle robot walking alongside.

"Ah, good timing. Natalie, this is Saskia Shiversand. I have personally assigned her to show you around the school and help you settle in."

Chapter Eight
CLASS

The moment that they were out of the headmaster's study Saskia stopped in the corridor and turned to look at Nat, eye-to-eye.

"Did you bring your sword with you?"

"Sword?" Nat frowned. "I don't have a sword."

Saskia pursed her lips. "Are you certain about that?"

Nat shrugged, opened her arms and cast them wide. "I am not carrying a sword. I don't own one either."

Saskia sniffed, turned on her heel and breezed off along the corridor with such authority that Nat wondered if she was a teacher instead of a pupil.

Other kids ducked out of her way as she dragged Nat up and down staircases, in and out of countless classrooms, lecture theatres, labs and sports halls.

She led, Nat followed. She didn't say anything else to her except "Your dragon is highly unusual", before pointing out they'd reached the chemistry department.

The school reminded Nat of her own in Hong Kong but it was much bigger, with grander rooms, larger sash windows and old-fashioned wooden furniture.

By the time they reached her year's floor, Nat found herself catching her breath from wearing such heavy clothes. She was used to Slider shorts and T-shirts, not corsets and long skirts.

"Your classroom," said Saskia, knocking on the door and opening it before anyone could reply.

The other kids were already sitting at their desks. There were four rows of boys and girls. Fifteen pairs of eyes turned to stare at Nat and Fizz, putting them in the spotlight.

A lesson was underway. The teacher was a thin lady with wire-framed glasses and a lace mob cap. Behind her, a wall screen showed a multicoloured map of the world.

"Thank you, Saskia," said the teacher.

Saskia turned to Nat.

"Any problems, get your dragon to call me. Mater's expecting us for tea promptly after school. Find me at the front entrance and we can ride together in my carriage," she said.

Carriage? Before she could reply Saskia swished her skirts around and flounced out of the classroom door.

"Everyone please welcome Natalie Walk—" began the teacher.

She was cut short by a loud *OINK!* Mr Limpet's pig came trotting in through the door, swiftly followed by the headmaster himself.

Every chair in the room scraped back on the tile floor as the whole class stood up to attention.

"Sit! Sit!" said Mr Limpet, waving a hand.

The chairs scraped again as everyone sat down. All eyes were fixed upon Nat. She wished the floor would open up and swallow her. Fizz moved in close. She could feel his snout brushing her ear.

Mr Limpet took hold of her by the elbow and steered her to the very front of the class next to the teacher. He cleared his throat with a loud *AHEM*!

"Now then, it gives me the greatest pleasure to introduce the newest member of our school. We are most honoured and privileged to welcome Natalie Walker into our midst. She has come all the way from Hong Kong. Her father was an old pupil of mine who went on to a stellar ascension in the world of computer gaming. The company he created is one that I know you will all recognise since most of you spend far too much time in its virtual world. Its name is SPIN."

There was a collective intake of breath.

"Indeed. The SPIN empire; worth a king's ransom. Sadly, Max Walker is no longer with us. He and

Natalie's mother departed our world in the most tragic of circumstances…"

The headmaster pulled a silk handkerchief from his top pocket and appeared to wipe away a tear. Nat blushed bright red. She wanted to run for the door, into the street and far, far away.

"However, let us put the fates to one side and look to the future."

Nat cringed as Mr Limpet grasped her hand, took a step backwards and held his other hand up like a circus ringmaster starting the show.

"We have been entrusted with the next generation of Walkers. I give you Natalie, SPIN heiress!"

Stunned silence from the classroom. So much for blending in. This was officially one of the most embarrassing moments in her life.

"I expect you all to make her most welcome here at Boxbury, embracing her into our midst. Thank you, and over to you, Professor Trogalming."

Mr Limpet let go of Nat's hand and swept out of the door, his pig trotting after him.

There was a stunned silence, before Professor Trogalming coughed and pointed at a line of old-fashioned lockers at the back of the room.

"Natalie," she said. "Please put your dragon over

there in your locker and take a seat at the spare desk in the back row. The rest of the class should focus back on the map as we continue with our study of mountain zones."

Nat fixed her eyes on the floor as she made her way through the rows of desks. She could sense that everyone was still staring at her. A flurry of low whispers darted around the room.

Professor Trogalming resumed her lesson.

Each locker had a split door, like a stable. The top of each one was open and a motley collection of robots had their heads stuck out. All had the Boxbury tie around their necks. She counted three rabbits, a hedgehog, two black Labradors, a couple of rats, a squirrel, a badger, an owl, a horse and two bears. She could see that most of them were from the Soyto "Fresh and Furry" line, just like Wen's rabbit robot, Fu. Even over here they were evidently the bestselling robots. All of them were in light sleep mode, their eyes half closed.

"*Why has that rat got those badges?*" whispered Fizz.

Nat peered closely at three blue oblong badges pinned to the rat's tie: "R-Prefect", "R-Runner", "R-Star".

The rat detected her looking. Its eyes popped open. It spread its lips into a big smile, showing bright yellow teeth.

"*The R denotes 'Robot'*," it whispered in a clipped English accent.

"*How do you acquire them?*" said Fizz, his eyes glowing bright amber.

"*Speak with me during break. I must sleep mode again.*"

It shut its eyes. Nat moved towards the end of the line to where her name was showing on a digital read-out label on the front of the bottom left locker. The one next to it read "Zixin Smith", but the locker looked empty.

She crouched down and lifted the latch. Inside, someone had carved their initials "LMJS" into the paintwork on the back of the door. Other than that it was bare.

"In you go," whispered Nat.

Fizz swooped off her shoulder into the locker. She closed the lower half of the door, but he was so much shorter than the other robots only the top of his head was showing through the upper opening.

"*It's dark and dismal in here,*" he said, his voice flat. A sudden lightning-quick flash of silver came shooting out of the next-door locker. A snake's head shot past her with an electric-blue forked tongue, its long, flat, chain-linked body whipping along behind. It slithered down into her locker.

A blast of smoke and flames erupted from her locker, followed by a loud hiss. She jumped out of the way. Someone started shrieking from the desks behind her.

"Miss Walker, will you please keep your dragon under control! You have your first warning and you've only been in my class for a few minutes," barked Professor Trogalming.

Nat turned to face the class. They were all staring at her again.

"I'm sorry, but a snake triggered his defence system."

Miss Trogalming held up a hand. "No excuses. Please take a seat."

Someone started to laugh. Tiger's teeth! She'd rather be having dinner with evil Aunt Vera than this. She glanced back at the locker. The snake's head was peeping over the top.

"*All is well. I am introducing myself,*" it hissed, before disappearing back inside.

"That's enough!" said Miss Trogalming. "Eyes back

to the screen, please, and take your seat immediately, Natalie."

Nat made her way over to the empty desk. She pulled back the wooden chair and sat down. Her desktop activated. The top slid up to form her screen, revealing a keypad and writing tablet below. The screen lit up with the map that was showing on the main screen. Her name was displayed in the top corner.

"Zixin, since Charlotte doesn't know the answer perhaps you can enlighten us," said Professor Trogalming.

"It's the Nilgiri, a range of mountains that forms a part of the Western Ghats," came the reply. It was slow, more of a drawl, and it was followed up with a yawn.

A green flag popped up on screen over the Himalayas. Nat turned to find that Zixin was her neighbour. He was sitting slouched back in his chair, evidently very bored. He wore the boys' uniform of long brown frock coat, high-collared white shirt and brown pinstripe trousers. He turned to meet her stare. He had black spiky hair with two stripes inked across each cheek. His brown eyes glazed over.

Then he opened his mouth and she nearly fell off

her chair in surprise. His tongue was forked. He grinned, flicking his tongue up and down just like his snake robot had done.

Chapter Nine
ZIXIN

The day went from bad to worse for Nat. She'd eaten lunch in the old dining room alone, with just Fizz for company. The others in her class sat in their cliques. Despite Mr Limpet's orders, they were all ignoring her.

Well, not completely ignoring her, since they kept looking over at her, their lips sneering as they used the word "heiress" again and again in their conversations. It was the worst day of her life, worse than anything that had happened to her in Mongolia.

When the final bell went she made her way through the bustling corridors towards the main entrance to meet Saskia. The school day was done and so was she.

Fizz was perched on her shoulder telling her how great his day had been hanging out with Vesperetta the snake. It made her feel even more miserable – her robot could fit in and have a great first day at school while hers was an epic disaster.

"Natalie!"

EMERALD SECRET

She slowed and turned to find Zixin running along the corridor towards her with Vesperetta slung around his neck.

He flicked his tongue out. She recoiled.

"Ah soz, didn't mean to, bad habit," he said, reaching her. "Congrats on surviving the day."

She'd sat next to him all day and he hadn't said a word to her. Maybe this was some kind of joke. She carried on making her way towards the main entrance to find Saskia.

"My mum was from Hong Kong."

She stopped and turned.

"Was?"

"Yeah. She died just after I was born. I never knew her. Dad brought me up."

"I'm sorry."

"What's it like?"

She frowned. "What? Being an *heiress*?"

She put a bitter emphasis on the last word.

"Nah, I meant what's Hong Kong like?"

"You've never been?"

He shuffled on his feet, awkward for a moment.

"Can't afford the airfare. I'm on a full scholarship at Boxbury. Got in with this," he said, tapping his head. "The others don't like me because I'm not like them.

I'm from the poor end of the city. Dad works on the Underground tube track maintenance. I don't fit in but that doesn't bother me. Don't let it bother you either."

Vesperetta had suspended herself across the gap between them and was hissing something into Fizz's ear. His eyes were glowing bright purple.

"Hong Kong is *ku*," said Nat. "Different from here."

"Want to go to Popko for a juice at the weekend?"

The very word made her taste buds tingle.

"Popko? There's one here in London?"

He raised his eyebrows. "Yeah, of course. Not in this area of town. Here it's all posh Victorian lemonade shop rubbish. It's over in my gaff, in the East End. I board here in the week, but can get out at weekends."

"*Saskia's poodle has just contacted me. She wants you to hurry up!*" announced Fizz.

"You know her?" said Zixin, frowning.

"No, but I've got to go home for tea with her today."

Zixin wrinkled his face up as if a nasty smell had wafted in on the breeze.

"She's the princess in WarZworld."

"WarZworld?"

Her mind was racing. Saskia played WarZworld?

The rival games company to SPIN.

"Yeah, her mum owns it. If you go into the game you'll find Miss Sassypants and her mates in there. They've built their own medieval kingdom. They like to torture all who enter."

"But you've got to be eighteen to play it."

Zixin shrugged. "Her mum's the boss. I get in it through a back door. Nasty place though. I prefer the games your dad built."

"She asked me earlier if I had my sword with me."

Zixin laughed. "She's been hanging out too long in WarZworld. You'd better get moving. Sassypants doesn't like to wait."

She smiled. His forked tongue might be weird, but he was the first, and only, person who'd been nice to her the whole day.

It was mayhem at the main entrance. Kids were pushing and shoving to get out through the double doors. Robots were barking, squawking and squeaking, while their owners jostled each other. Nat slipped into the flow around the side and was about to step out of the school when Fizz tapped her with his claw.

"Hat must be on. Vesperetta said you'll get a warning if a security guard or teacher sees you. Zixin received

two warnings and then got a detention. Vesperetta
said he had to wear his top hat in lessons and while he
was playing football for a whole week."

She groaned, and crammed it on to her head.
"*Zoinks*, please just cut the 'Vesperetta said' thing."

Fizz snorted. "*I am only trying to assist you.*"

Out in the road a long queue of Grooveriders and
Overriders had formed. They were all high-end with
mirror-polished paintwork and blacked-out windows.
The low-slung Grooveriders fitted into the
cityscape with their crouching, panther-like design.
But the massive, all-terrain Overriders with over-
sized knobbly tyres looked out of place. They were
great for places in the wild, like on the Steppe in
Mongolia, but in a very busy city, with narrow streets,
they looked like elephants in a mouse maze.

A gust of wind rustled the leaves in the trees
overhead. Nat felt her hat start to tug away. She
gripped on to the brim to stop it flying off.

"Where is she?" she said.

Fizz's eyes flashed red as he scanned the crowds.

"*Saskia and the poodle are in the carriage,*" he said,
pointing his snout over to the far side of the square.

"*Zoinks!*" said Nat, spotting a massive black carriage
decorated with golden swords.

EMERALD SECRET

Four gleaming grey horses were harnessed up to the front with plumes of scarlet ostrich feathers in their headbands. A driver wearing a suit of armour was standing holding the reins. Nat had never seen anything like it in real life.

She dodged through the crowd and hobbled across the square in her heavy skirt.

"About time," grumbled Saskia, who was sitting inside on a royal-blue velvet seat, her poodle lying next to her.

"Sorry," said Nat, climbing in.

She took a seat opposite Saskia. The door closed automatically and immediately the hum of the city vanished. The carriage was a soundproof box on wheels.

"Good day?" said Saskia.

Nat wasn't sure how to reply. If Wen or her cousin Henry were asking she'd say, "*Ai yah!* Worst day ever. Worse than being bitten by a giant centipede." But she didn't know Saskia, and so far the other girl wasn't being very friendly.

She wondered again why she'd been asked to tea. Most likely it was Mr Limpet who'd set it up.

"I'm glad it's over," she said.

Saskia nodded. She was staring at Nat, her arctic-blue eyes boring into her.

"Your dragon is unusual. Who made him?"

Nat's hand shot up to where Fizz was perched on her shoulder.

"My dad. He designed him for me. Fizz was activated when I was born."

"How long have you been an orphan?" Saskia continued to stare at her.

How Nat hated that word! It lived in the dark shadows of her mind. She looked out of the carriage window. They were rolling along the street now at a fast clip. It was surprising how quickly four horses could pull such a big carriage along.

"Since I was two. Mum and Dad died in a plane crash."

"Who looks after you then?"

More Miss Nosy than Sassypants.

"Jamuka." She wouldn't give any more detail than that.

"Ah…" Saskia trailed off. "Did you know that my mother and your father were at Boxbury together?"

Chapter Ten
SHIVERSAND TOWERS

The carriage pulled off the street through a massive set of wrought-iron gates and into a circular driveway. Nat looked out of the window. A huge horse statue with a bronze warrior queen on its back was rearing up in the centre of a stone fountain, frozen in time. In her hands she held a spear and shield. She had long hair down to her waist and was wearing some sort of warrior-queen bikini. Water was spurting out in a high arc from the end of the spear.

If Wen had been there, she'd have giggled and called it "*unding*".

"That's Mater when she started WarZworld," said Saskia. "She was Boudicca, Queen of the Iceni tribe. William Duncton made her sit for two days while he sculpted her."

Saskia hadn't said anything more about their parents being at school together. She said Mater would want that pleasure, but if this statue was anything like the real Ivy Shiversand, Nat was officially dreading meeting her.

The carriage came to a stop. The door swung open automatically and Saskia led the way down. Nat followed, her lace-up leather boots pinching her toes as she landed on the gravel below. In front of her, at the top of a wide flight of marble steps, loomed a building that looked more like a hotel than a house. The words "Shiversand Towers" were carved into the stone above a double-fronted glass doorway.

"Hurry. Mater doesn't like to be kept waiting!" said Saskia, snapping her fingers.

Nat had a sudden urge to take a flying kick through the air to the back of Saskia's head. Better not.

Their boots echoed across the marble entrance hall. Saskia removed her hat and tossed it on to an eagle sculpture that was suspended from a wall. A heavy crystal chandelier hung from a central pendant, throwing bright light across the room.

Nat glanced up and gawped. The ceiling was covered in an oil mural of Saskia's mother in her warrior bikini, this time at the reins of a golden chariot.

"*Zoinks!* Film this and send it to Wen," she whispered to Fizz.

Fizz lifted his snout up and started to scan across the ceiling.

EMERALD SECRET

"*STOP!*" barked the poodle, making them both jump.

It came trotting over, growling. Nat took a step backwards but Fizz leapt into protect mode. He swooped down off her shoulder, blasting a plume of smoke right into the poodle's eyes.

It snarled, curling back its lips to reveal a full set of pristine "*Sharper Than The Sharpest Samurai Sword*" teeth. Nat gulped. She'd only seen teeth like that in a kung fu movie where the hero had had to fight off a crazed rat robot. The hero won, but not before the rat had nearly bitten off his arm, its sword-edged teeth slicing through the skin with ease.

"Poxo, stop it! Come!" shouted Saskia from down the hallway.

The poodle narrowed its eyes, snapped its jaws shut and obeyed her command. Nat turned to leave. She'd had enough. She didn't need Miss Sassypants or her sword-teeth poodle. She'd find a taxi and go home to the *Junko*.

"*Miss Walker, how nice to meet you. Please follow me.*"

She looked around her, searching for the owner of the squeaky voice.

"*Down below,*" Fizz whispered in her ear.

The beetlebot that had delivered the invitation at the dock the day before was standing at her feet. Its compound beetle eyes were flashing, its antennae twitching. Even though she knew it was a robot, it still made her skin crawl.

"*This way, please.*"

It scuttled off across the marble floor in the same direction as Saskia. Nat hesitated, wondering what to do – should she leave or not?

"*It would be impolite not to follow,*" said Fizz.

"*Zoula!*" said Nat. "We're not staying long though. If I tap you on your wing, you must announce in a loud voice that you've had a message from Jamuka saying we are needed back at the *Junko* straight away."

"*That would make me a liar.*"

A wave of tiredness washed over her. Sometimes she wished Fizz was how he used to be before his upgrade – a yes/no, "do as I command", typical robot.

"Please, just do it for me this once."

"*Yes, my lady.*" He swept a wing across his chest and made a short bow.

They followed the beetlebot into a hallway lined with glass cases filled with ancient weapons – swords, bows and arrows, daggers and axes. A low, constant drumbeat was playing through hidden speakers.

At the end they entered a large wood-panelled room lit by flickering candles. An old oil painting of a castle covered one wall and lattice-paned windows let in the grey light of the afternoon. A pair of suits of armour flanked a fireplace. It was like walking into an ancient castle.

Towards the centre of the room stood a golden throne. Nat gasped. A large woman with a chalk-white face and a mass of jet-black, gold-streaked hair, dressed in armour, was occupying it. The beetlebot was crawling up the woman's arm, coming to rest on her shoulder plate.

"*Scary,*" whispered Fizz.

"Natalie, welcome! Come and say hello," said the woman, her voice low and booming.

"*Ooh! That's a very posh English accent.*"

Fizz was leaning in so close that his snout was sticking in Nat's ear. She twitched and made her way over. Saskia was standing near the windows, arms crossed, watching Nat's progress, her menacing poodle sitting to attention at her side.

Nat reached the throne. She wasn't certain whether to bow, kneel or what to do. Ivy extended a sweaty hand.

"I am delighted to meet you at last," she said. "I am Baroness Shiversand, but do call me Ivy."

They shook hands. *Zoinks!* How could this be the same warrior queen of the fountain and hall ceiling? It was as if she'd been inflated with a balloon pump to five times her normal size. She was spilling over the sides of her throne. Her Spiderwire armour was stretched thin at the seams. It had to be really uncomfortable to wear.

A suffocating waft of stale sweat hit Nat's nostrils, along with something else that she couldn't quite figure out. It wasn't the perfume-fug that Aunt Vera emitted. It was more like mothballs. She wrinkled her nose. Mothballs and sweat.

Ivy waved at a small footstool at her feet.

"Please, do take a seat."

She obeyed. This wasn't the kind of woman you said no to. Tiger's teeth, the woman's skin was waxy! Maybe she was really dead. Maybe she was a robot.

A loud farting sound came from the throne.

"That's better," said Ivy, not apologising.

A smell like a hundred-year-old egg spread out from the throne. Nat wrinkled her nose again. OK, Ivy was definitely alive.

"Mater, where's the tea?" said Saskia.

Nat looked from Saskia to the baroness. It was like they were both out of history books but ones on completely different eras. Saskia was Victorian; her mother medieval.

She wondered how her dad could have been at school at the same time as Ivy. Surely if he was alive he wouldn't look like some bloated, worn-out warrior – he'd be strong, young and tiger-like?

"Tea is on its way, Saskia. Now, Natalie. We have much to—"

A butler walked in pushing a three-tier tea trolley. China teacups rattled as he wheeled it across the polished floor. There were enough cakes and sandwiches to feed a dozen people. He parked it next to Ivy's throne.

Saskia hurried over, grabbed a slice of cake and made her way swiftly towards the door.

"Back soon, going to get changed," was all she said before disappearing, leaving Nat alone with Ivy.

Ivy handed Nat a plate.

"Do help yourself," she said, smearing jam and a huge dollop of clotted cream on to a scone and cramming it into her mouth.

Nat took a slice of cake. The yellow icing was so

thick her fingers sank into the sticky mass.

"You are so like your father," said Ivy, her left eyelid flickering as if she was trying to wink.

Chapter Eleven
THE SWORD

Nat put the cake on her plate. She looked at the gloopy icing that had glued itself to her fingers and wondered what she was meant to do. There were no napkins, and she didn't want to lick her fingers because Ivy was doing the very same thing with the jam and clotted cream, and it was putting her off.

All the time she was thinking about her dad, of the photo of him standing in uniform outside Boxbury.

Apart from her dad's half brother, Uncle Fergal, who never talked about him, she'd never met anyone who knew her dad from so long ago.

"Were you friends?" she asked.

Ivy snorted. "More rivals than friends. We were Boxbury's champion geeks. I was faster at coding; your father was better at system design."

She nodded at Fizz, who was perched on Nat's shoulder.

"My guess is that he designed your robot. I assume it flies, blows smoke and flames, and used to hum

'Flower of Scotland' to you when you were a baby."

The plate fell out of Nat's hand and crashed to the floor. How could Ivy know about that tune? That was her secret, not to be shared with anyone, especially Ivy Shiversand.

She reached down to pick up the smashed plate but two beetlebots were ahead of her, sweeping bits of cake and plate into a pile. At least she wouldn't have to eat it now.

"How do you know all that?"

"Because he designed a dragon robot for a year-end project. Just like the one on your shoulder. He was always fascinated by dragons. He'd spend hours drawing what he considered to be the perfect one. He won the Boxbury computer prize for it, beating me for once. Mine was for a poodle robot. I had it created for Saskia when she was born."

Rats' tails, she was lucky her dad had liked dragons. She could have ended up with a scissor-teethed poodle.

"We went on to UCL together," said Ivy.

"Where?"

"University College London. We were on the virtual reality science degree course."

"Did you know my mum then?"

Ivy jolted in her throne as if she'd been given an

electric shock. Her eyes popped wide and her lips pursed up.

"It was after that when your parents met."

Nat frowned. She thought they had still been students when they met.

"I was told they'd met here in London."

Ivy took a loud slurp of tea and burped.

"PhD, both of them. Cath—" She stopped and coughed, unable to get Nat's mum's name out. "—erine, your mother, was at SOAS. That was after we'd graduated."

So Ivy did know her mum. "What were they like?"

Ivy grabbed a sandwich and ate it in one gulp.

"It was a long time ago. I hardly knew her at all."

The butler cleared his throat noisily from the doorway.

"Excuse me, ma'am. The Bateleys man is here."

Ivy waved her hand.

"Perfect timing. Bring him in."

A man in a long brown apron with a blue and gold "B" embroidered on the pocket walked in carrying a long wooden crate. A second later Poxo came flying through the door behind him, skidding on the floor, growling and snapping at the man's heels, teeth glinting. The Bateleys man froze on the spot.

"Poxo, go back upstairs!" roared Ivy.

The poodle stopped, whimpered and retreated.

"Thanks," said the Bateleys man. "My mate said to watch out for him."

"Come. Bring it here," said Ivy, pushing herself up off the throne.

Nat decided to stand up too and move out of the way. The man reached Ivy and went down on one knee, offering the crate up from gloved hands.

"Baroness Shiversand. Lot two hundred and eighty-three," he announced. "Would you like me to open it for you?"

Ivy grabbed it off him. "That won't be necessary. You can take your leave."

He was up and out of the room in a flash. Nat was thinking she'd like to do the same thing.

"Sit, Natalie."

It was a command. Nat scowled, but took her seat again at Ivy's feet.

"*She thinks herself a queen,*" whispered Fizz. "*Shall I announce that we must leave?*"

Ivy flopped back down on her throne with the crate across her vast lap. She unfastened the clips and lifted the lid.

"This is over three thousand years old," she said,

lifting out a red silk-covered box.

"Not yet. I want to see what's inside," said Nat, so softly only Fizz could hear.

Ivy took a deep breath, opened the box and pulled out an ancient, rusty sword by the handle. She swept it up into the air.

"I presume you are familiar with this kind of thing, Natalie?" said Ivy, running a sweaty finger across the surface of the blade.

Nat shook her head. Why did Saskia and Ivy think she had a sword?

Ivy narrowed her eyes, bringing the blade of the sword down to Nat's eye level. Fizz snorted out a plume of smoke, lifted a talon and with a clang of metal-on-metal pushed the blade away from Nat.

"*Too close, remove the weapon!*" he announced.

Ivy tittered with laughter and placed the sword on her lap.

"Max Walker's defence robot. I bet you do kung fu, don't you?"

That was it. Time to leave. Nat didn't like this woman one bit. She jumped up.

"It's late. I must head home," she said.

Ivy cocked her head to one side.

"Indulge me for just a few more minutes and I will tell you more about your father."

Her dad. Of course she wanted to know more.

"Did your parents leave you anything like this?" said Ivy, her hand stroking the blade of the sword.

"No."

"No mention of any sword in their will?"

"No. Why?"

What was Ivy getting at? There were no swords anywhere on the *Junko*. The only weapon she had was Fizz.

"Did your mother leave you any papers about a sword and a crown?"

"No. Why would she?"

Ivy leaned over the sword, closer in to Nat.

"Did you know your mother was an expert on ancient weaponry?"

Nat had no idea what she was talking about.

Saskia came sweeping in, dressed in another full-length hooped dress. The pattern was grey and white like a snow leopard. "Poxo said the sword's arrived. We've brought the crown."

The poodle held the strings of a large velvet pouch between his teeth.

"Excellent. Lower the blinds. Move to one side,

Natalie, and observe."

Nat moved out of the way as fast as her heavy uniform would allow.

The window blinds automatically began to lower. A spotlight over the throne switched on, bathing Ivy in its harsh beam, highlighting her wild hair and scary-looking face.

"Ready, Mater?"

Ivy nodded. Saskia took the pouch from Poxo and tugged open the strings. She pulled out a glittering gold crown studded with rubies. Ivy lifted the sword up, pointing its blade to the heavens. She closed her eyes.

"*Boÿuÿdika rigani jowant briga,*" she chanted.

Saskia repeated the phrase, lifting the crown up high and approaching her mother.

Ivy's nostrils flared. She chanted the phrase again. Nat tapped Fizz on his wing.

"*My massive processing power and knowledge base is struggling with a translation,*" he said, pressing his snout into her ear.

"A rough idea would be good," she whispered.

Ivy and Saskia were now chanting in duet.

"*I don't do rough ideas, but I can say that the closest approximation is to the ancient proto-Celtic language, but based on the construction of the sentence I am not sure…"*

"Just say it," said Nat, listening to them chanting it faster, their voices raised.

"Boÿuÿdika rigani jowant briga *roughly means: 'victorious queen youth power'.*"

Saskia now held the crown directly above Ivy's head. Both mother and daughter stopped chanting. Saskia lowered it slowly until it was set upon her mother's head. She carefully removed her hands, bowed her head and took a step backwards. From inside a pocket in her dress she produced a pearl-framed mirror and held it up in front of Ivy's face, but Ivy kept her eyes firmly closed.

Tiger's teeth, this was weird! They were like a pair of royal statues – the queen and the princess. There wasn't a sound in the room.

Nat didn't dare whisper anything to Fizz in case she was heard. She replayed everything Ivy had said about her parents, especially her mum. If her mum had been an expert on ancient weaponry, then why didn't Nat know that? And what was this sword and crown thing all about?

After what seemed like longer than waiting for a snail to cross the road, Ivy's eyelids lifted. She looked at herself in the mirror, and growled, "No!"

Saskia averted her gaze to the floor. "It is not the one, Mater."

Ivy swept the mirror out of Saskia's hands. It crashed to the floor, shattering into a thousand shards. She took a huge intake of breath and drew her other arm backwards.

"*Duck!*" said Fizz, his snout flashing red.

Nat threw herself to the floor as the sword flew out of Ivy's hand and whizzed overhead like an arrow. It passed straight through the canvas oil painting of the castle with a loud ripping sound. The tip pinged off the flex-diamond screen behind, and clattered on to the wooden floor.

"Arrrrrghhhhhhhhhh!" screamed Ivy, standing up from her throne and beating her armour chest plate with her fists.

"*Zoula!*" said Nat.

She leapt to her feet, hitched up her skirt and sprinted out of the room as fast as her legs could carry her.

Chapter Twelve
JAMUKA

Nat didn't stop running until her boots landed on the deck of the *Junko*. Fizz was flying along just in front of her. He'd navigated the shortest road route back to St Katharine Docks and was now opening the boat's main hatch so that she could run straight inside.

She found Jamuka in the kitchen galley drinking Vietnamese weasel coffee and frowning at his FastPad. Gobi spotted Fizz and started chirping at him from her cage.

"*Ai yah!* This has been the worst day ever," she said, tossing her hat on to the galley counter.

Nat kicked off her boots and pulled off her jacket and skirt. The pintucked white shirt reached her knees like a dress.

Ah Ping had left a jug of cherry juice out. She poured some into a glass and gulped it down in one go. Jamuka still hadn't looked up from his FastPad.

"Hellloooo!" she said, tapping him on the shoulder.

He jumped and looked up over his half-moon glasses.

"Bao Bao! Sorry, I was watching Dragon Khan's last race."

"Today was worse than being put in a box full of snakes. Please can we go back home?" she said.

Jamuka took off his glasses and rubbed the bridge of his nose.

"*This* is our home for the next two years. The first day at a new school is often the hardest."

"It's not the school. I hate it, but it wasn't as bad as tea with the baroness. Even though she knows – I mean, knew – Mum and Dad!"

Jamuka frowned.

"She was at Boxbury with Dad. She was a geek just like him, but she's mad. She runs WarZworld and thinks she's a QUEEN! I had to watch her weird crowning ceremony with some ancient sword."

Jamuka's hand shot out. He squeezed her arm.

"Wait! Slow down. You said a sword?"

She stopped. His eyes were now fixed on hers.

"Yes, some ancient sword. She said Mum knew all about ancient swords. Did she?"

He didn't reply straight away. Instead he turned to her little dragon.

"Fizz, activate a full security sweep on board and close all access points including portholes."

"*Aye aye, Captain*," he said, saluting with his wing before flying out of the kitchen.

The two portholes whirred closed above the sink.

"*Zoinks*, Jamuka, what are you doing?"

Jamuka held his finger to his lips. He took her hand and headed for the door. Nat followed him, her heart thudding, as he lead her to the dojo. They sat down, cross-legged, in the centre of the mat.

The door opened. Fizz tiptoed in, his talons making light rasping sounds as he crossed the jigsaw matting to where they were sitting. He climbed up Nat's arm and perched on her shoulder, nuzzling his warm snout into the nape of her neck.

"*Perimeter is secured*," he announced.

"Thank you," said Jamuka. "Now, Bao Bao, you and Fizz need to tell me everything that happened from the moment you left Boxbury with Saskia."

Nat opened her mouth to speak but was stopped short by a loud snort from Fizz.

"*I have a confession to make.*"

"How very human of you, Fizz," said Jamuka.

Fizz's eyes flashed purple. "*I decided to film everything from the moment we left Boxbury using my Stealth-System X150."*

Nat turned to look at him on her shoulder.

"Your what?"

He swooped down on to the mat, opened his wings and activated his screen.

"My Stealth-System X150. I downloaded it from Spytastic three days ago on a trial basis. I thought I'd give it a go, and then convince you to purchase the full version, including the night-vision option."

Poxo's poodle head appeared, filling the screen. In the background Saskia could be heard, asking her nosy questions.

"I started using it to check out the poodle. It can't do as much as me."

Nat felt a surge of love for her dragon. *Zoinks*, he was clever. She reached down and patted his head. He looked up at her, his snout and eyes blazing purple. At least they were in this together.

The film cut off when they exited Shiversand Towers' gates at top speed. Jamuka got to his feet and started to pace up and down the mat, his head bent low, hands clasped behind his back.

"Your mother was an ancient-weaponry expert; that was how she met your father. She was lecturing at SOAS here in London. Your father attended her lecture. It was love at first sight."

"But you said they met at a party."

"That was because they wanted to protect you, until the time was right."

Nat frowned. "From what? Until what?"

Jamuka stopped pacing and stood looking out across the dock.

"From this kind of thing. I must go to Shiversand Towers now and sort this out."

"Sort what out?"

He turned round to face Nat.

"The sword Ivy's searching for. She wants it for the wrong reason. It'll never do what she wants. I need to tell her that. I need her to leave you alone."

He was striding towards the door.

"I'll come with you," Nat said, following him into the corridor.

He stopped at the main hatch and turned to her.

"This is something I must do alone, Bao Bao. I'll be back later. Fizz, keep the *Junko* secured."

He put his arms around Nat and gave her a hug.

"There is much I must teach you. But not yet."

Chapter Thirteen
FAIRYTAIL

"*Wen is calling*," announced Fizz, tapping her on the shoulder with his talon.

Nat opened her eyes. She must have fallen asleep on her bunk. Her cabin was bathed in a yellow glow from the dockside light that was shining in through the window.

"Take it," she said, yawning.

Fizz hopped around on her pillow and spread his wings. Wen appeared on the screen along with Nat's cousin Henry. Both of them were in Weiwood school uniform, sitting at the marble-topped kitchen counter at Wen's house on The Peak. Behind them, through the panoramic window, she could see clear blue sky, sunshine and the tips of the sea of skyscrapers that were clustered down below in the Central District. She wished she were with them.

Henry's freckled face leaned into the camera.

"Are you still in bed?" he asked.

Wen shoved him out of the way.

"*Ai yah!* Of course she is. I told you about the time difference in London. It's the middle of the night. We are waking her up."

Henry tapped his squirrel robot's nose. NutNut flicked his tail, held up a Union Jack, opened his mouth and began to sing the national anthem.

Wen reached over, grabbed NutNut and twisted his ear. The squirrel shut his mouth and the music came to a stop.

"Hey, I taught NutNut that specially for Nat!"

Nat smiled. She hadn't spoken with Henry for a few days because he'd had to go on a trip to Shanghai with Uncle Fergal and Prissy. They'd been to collect Aunt Vera from her clinic, and no robots had been allowed.

"Thanks, Henry."

"I agree, it is nice," said Wen, ruffling Henry's red hair. "But ... hang on."

She picked up a can of "Concreter Hairspray", aimed it at the front quiff she'd created with his fringe and blasted it with spray.

Henry pushed her away and started coughing from the fug.

"That's *ding*," said Wen, admiring her own work. "I'll make you fashionable yet, Henry Walker."

She looked back into camera.

"Now, on to the serious business of the hour. We've watched the Fizz film, and who is that crazy queen and her daughter? Is this some kind of dramedy show you've shot?"

"No, it's not, it's real."

Wen and Henry looked at each other, looked back at Nat and both leaned into camera searching Nat's face for a hint of a smile.

"It's not a joke?" said Henry.

"No. No joke. It's real."

Silence.

"That queen, the sword, crown, girl dressed like Mary Poppins, it's all really real?" said Wen.

"Yes. It seems there's something to do with my parents and a sword and it's all hush-hush secret. Jamuka's gone over to the crazy queen's house to talk to her about it."

Wen whistled. Henry frowned.

"I wish we were with you," he said.

"Me too," said Nat. "Or, I wish I'd never had to come here and I was still in Hong Kong with you. *Zoinks!* Jamuka says he's loads to teach me but not yet. And I don't even know what's planned for me then. In the meantime I've got to go to a school where no one speaks to me because the headmaster has told them all I'm some special heiress—"

"*Ahem*," interrupted Fizz in a posh English accent. "*Not quite no one. We have both formed acquaintances, myself with Vesperetta and you with Zixin.*"

"*Ding* accent, Fizz! I must download that for Fu. Do they make it for Super Fresh and Furry robots?" said Wen.

"*I'll send you the—*"

"Stop!" said Nat. "This is serious. That's why I sent you the film. My life is big, major, massive pants."

"At least you haven't got my mum," said Henry. "Even though she's been in the clinic, or sanatorium as she calls it, for months, she's not really come back any nicer. I think she's even more grumpy. She stays in all the time, won't go out anywhere and says it's because we're poor."

An image of Aunt Vera screaming across the courtroom at her flashed through Nat's mind.

"True. But my parents are running my life from the grave. Why can't I just be left alone?"

Wen shrugged. "I don't know, Nat. Make Jamuka tell you the truth. It sounds as if he'll need to if people like the crazy queen are after you. Who are

Vesperetta and Zixin?"

"Vesperetta is a robot snake. She belongs to this boy, Zixin, who sits next to me in class. He's got a weird, forked tongue."

"*Ding!* Send me a picture, please."

A loud ringing echoed across Wen's kitchen. Henry groaned.

"School. Do we have to go?" he moaned.

Wen jumped down off her stool.

"Yes we do, right now, otherwise I'll get detention again."

She picked her Slider helmet up and put it on.

"Like the new paint job?" said Wen, modelling it for the camera.

Nat laughed. Her friend had printed out the blue and gold Boxbury school crest with the pig's head and stuck it on the front. Henry was wearing his helmet now. He'd got the same paint job.

"We wanted to make sure you didn't feel alone," he said.

She gave them a thumbs-up.

"I hope Jamuka sorts it all out. Remember to get him to tell you the truth. You deserve to know. *ZOULA!* Over and out," said Wen, cutting the call.

Nat yawned and moved down her bunk to rest her

head on her pillow.

"I'm as tired as a million-year-old dog. Wake me up at seven, please, Fizz."

"*Affirmative, my lady.*"

But she was awake again by five. Fizz was in power-down sleep mode so she decided to leave him and have a moment to herself.

She walked on to the deck to find it shrouded in a layer of fog. She could hear the mournful squawk of seagulls flying overhead, and the low roar of early morning traffic crossing Tower Bridge.

The large brass clock on the main dock warehouse chimed. She looked at the upper deck expecting to see Jamuka sitting cross-legged, deep in his morning meditation, but it was deserted. He must still be asleep. She shivered in her thin, tiger-print pyjamas. If London was this cold now she dreaded to think what winter was going to be like. No wonder her parents had moved to Hong Kong.

She reached back inside the hatch, unhooked Jamuka's grey Mongolian coat off a peg and pulled it on. The soft fur lining warmed her skin.

A smell of freshly baked bread wafted over the water, making her stomach growl. Breakfast. She checked the pockets of the coat and her fingers curled around a handful of English coins. Perfect, no need to wake Fizz to come with her to pay. She could go on her own, no questions, no chatting.

She started to walk across the deck towards the gangway but as her feet met with the damp, fog-slicked planks she realised she'd forgotten to put on her boots. She turned to head back to the cabin, when she caught sight of the top of the launch dinghy. Perfect, no shoes required. She crossed to the rail, climbed over and jumped aboard.

The cables whirred into action, lowering the dinghy. It hit the murky water with a splash. She took hold of the tiller and twisted. The motor purred into action, propelling her forward.

"*Wait for me!*"

She looked up and sighed. Fizz, his emerald-green wings fully spread, was flying towards her at top speed. He swooped down, coming in to land on her shoulder.

"*Where are we going?*"

Nat slowed the motor.

"Here."

Fizz put his snout up into the air and inhaled.

"*Yeast, flour, salt, sugar baked at one hundred and eighty degrees centigrade.*"

"Don't ruin it for me."

She picked up the mooring rope, tied it to a metal ladder set into the wall and climbed up to the quay. The cobbles were cold and slippery. She dashed across them to the bakery, the long coat dragging behind her. The bell on the bakery door tinkled as she ran inside. The woman behind the counter looked up and smiled.

"Morning! You look like you've come out of a fairytale."

Nat caught sight of herself in the mirror opposite. Her red hair was unbrushed, slept on, wild. She'd got Fizz perched on her shoulder, and Jamuka's coat looked like some medieval cloak.

She blushed with embarrassment, feeling out of place, alien again. The woman fished out a warm croissant from the counter, placed it on a napkin and handed it to her.

"It's on the house. We were inundated with hungry tourists yesterday who were here just to see your boat."

Nat smiled and bowed her head. "Thank you."

The woman looked out of the window across the dock. "So what's all the grey stuff on it? You trying to hide?"

Nat followed her gaze. From where they were

standing the *Junko* looked unreal, more of a ghost boat than a real one.

"We want to fit in, be below the radar. It's a security blanket."

The woman chuckled and raised an eyebrow. "You've got a green dragon on your shoulder, you look like a medieval princess and you live on an ancient ship. Fit in, you say?"

Chapter Fourteen
DARK DAY

Nat finished her yoghurt and fruit and made her way along the corridor to Jamuka's cabin. It wasn't often that he slept in past dawn. She knocked lightly but when there was no answer she quietly turned the handle and peeped inside. He was lying on his bunk under his blankets, his head on the pillow facing away from her.

"Jamuka," she called softly. But he didn't answer.

She guessed he must have got in very late from Shiversand Towers. She closed the door. She'd have to call him during first break to find out what had happened.

She headed up onto the deck to where Fizz was waiting, perched on her custom-built turquoise Slider board.

"*Are you ready to mount your steed?*" he said, activating the power.

The board's taillights flashed electric blue, the tiger's-head design on the top glowed bright orange.

EMERALD SECRET

It lifted up off the deck, coming to a hover at knee height.

"That's not funny," Nat said, hitching up her skirt to climb onboard.

The whole Victorian thing was getting on her nerves. Why someone like Saskia would want to wear this style of clothes when she wasn't even at school made her mind boggle.

She reached over and touched the tip of the handlebars set into the board. They raised up and clicked into place.

She stepped up and felt the magnets in her Slider boots connect and lock her feet to the board. She'd stuffed her school boots into the Boxbury carpet bag that was slung across her back. The Slider sensed her weight. The neon-yellow tracking lights lit up around the board's edges and a dashboard popped up out of the handlebars.

She crammed her top hat over her hair, which had frizzed up in the early morning fog. As per Boxbury's instructions she pinched the brim. A chinstrap spooled out and wrapped under her chin.

"Not a good look at all, very *un-ding*," she grumbled, thinking of the cool Boxbury crest paint job that Wen and Henry had done to their helmets.

"*Tally ho!*" said Fizz, flying up and wrapping his talons around the handlebars.

"*Zoula!*" Nat pushed the handlebars forward. The Slider glided up into the air, over the railing and down on to the dock.

She slowly weaved her way through a stream of commuters, down a cobbled alleyway and out into a Slider lane.

"*Navigation set for Soho Square, but the most direct route is jammed. Searching for alternative,*" announced Fizz.

The navigation system switched to a new route that estimated an extra ten minutes of travel time. She pushed the handlebars further forward. The Slider picked up speed and she whizzed past the ancient stone walls of the Tower of London. It felt good to be outside, moving along at a clip.

Once past the Tower she had to turn into a main city Slider lane. The lane she was coming out of had been really quiet in comparison. She paused at the junction, watching Sliders whizzing by at top speed. Men and women in top hats and suits were flying by. A few kids around her age in school uniform were also travelling at speed. Robots of all shapes and sizes were sitting on handlebars. There were a few people in modern clothes among them all. They were on older Sliders, unable to keep up with the rest.

It was so congested in Hong Kong that the Slider speed limit was set to cruise level or below. Here, though, it didn't look like there were any restrictions. She took a deep breath.

"*Zoula*," she said to herself, and moved into the lane.

"Out of the way!" shouted a man riding a grey Slider, buzzing close by and cutting in front of her.

She moved over, but another and another rider zipped past at top speed.

"*Ai yah!* They're like ninja demons," she exclaimed.

Nat was soon fed up with being jostled and nearly run out of her lane. She pushed the handlebars further forward. The Slider started to shift up through its speed levels. Hers was the latest top-of-the-line X888 board. Ever since she'd had it she'd never ridden it at level seven or above, but here in the fast lanes of London she found herself at level nine, dodging in and out and around the traffic. With more power than most of the others in the lane, she was soon on the tail of the grey Slider that had cut her off.

She accelerated up to max level ten. The Slider surged forward. She leaned to the right, whipped out and around the grey Slider.

"Out of the way!" she shouted at the man, forcing him to move across.

She zoomed ahead of him.

"*That was a petty and dangerous manoeuvre*," shouted Fizz, who was hunkered down over the handlebars with his snout stuck out and his wings firmly clasped to his sides.

Nat didn't care. It had made her feel a lot better.

But when she pulled into Soho Square and spotted the Boxbury school crest on the road sign, all her euphoria evaporated. Day two was about to start.

She was just turning down the ramp into the underground Slider park when a Boxbury security guard came running across the pavement waving his arms at her to stop.

She pulled back on the handlebars, bringing her Slider to hover mode.

"I'll take your Slider from here, Miss Walker. Mr Limpet would like to see you in his study straight away."

What did Limpet want? She was now dreading day two more than she had a second ago. The guard held out his hand to help her get down but she ignored him and jumped off. She didn't need anyone's help.

EMERALD SECRET

"*OINK! Follow me, please,*" said Limpet's pig robot, arriving at her side.

It started trotting off towards the main entrance.

"Why does he want to see me?" she asked.

The pig replied with only a brief "*OINK!*" before continuing on its way. The tide of pupils parted as the pig passed along the school corridor. Nat could hear them whispering about "the heiress" when they spotted her in tow.

Mr Limpet was standing by the fireplace with his back to her when she entered his study. The pig closed the door behind her before oinking her presence to him.

He turned. His face looked crumpled, ashen.

"Natalie, please take a seat," he said, waving towards a leather armchair.

She walked across the rug and sat down.

"I have some bad news, I'm afraid. Your boatkeeper, Miss Ah Ping, called as she has been unable to wake your guardian this morning. It seems that Mr Borjigin passed away in the night. I'm so very sorry."

Chapter Fifteen
RETURN TO THE JUNKO

By the time the school's Grooverider had pulled up next to the *Junko* there was a sea of blue flashing lights at the bottom of the gangplank. Two police cars, an ambulance and a green cross doctor's car were parked up, along with a growing crowd of onlookers.

Nat wrenched opened the door.

"Wait," said Mr Limpet, trying to stop her, but she was already out, sprinting up the gangplank with Fizz flying at her side.

A local news reporter shouted out to her for an interview. She was oblivious. She had to get to Jamuka's cabin as fast as possible and properly wake him up.

She was halfway along the below-deck corridor when a policewoman stepped into her path.

"Wait, ple—"

But Nat dodged around her. A policeman was on guard outside Jamuka's cabin door. She ducked underneath him.

EMERALD SECRET

A woman wearing a white hazmat suit and rubber gloves was standing over Jamuka's empty bunk holding a pair of tweezers in one hand and a test tube in another.

"Where is he? What have you done with Jamuka!" she cried.

A pair of hands grasped hold of her arms and pulled her back.

"No!!!!!"

She turned and took out the policeman with a high kick, knocking him across the cabin.

"Ouf!" he cried, falling to the cabin floor.

Nat ran towards the empty bunk.

"Where is he?" she cried, choking up in panic.

She felt a sharp jab in her arm.

"Ouch!"

Her knees buckled. She collapsed to the cabin floor and blacked out.

Chapter Sixteen
THE GUARDIANS

The pitter-patter of rain on the porthole woke Nat up. She opened her eyes. A fresh breeze was blowing in off the water.

She was on her bunk, under a duvet. She shifted her head on the pillow. Her neck was stiff. A dull, throbbing ache pulsed through her body.

"*You're awake*," said Fizz from his perch at the end of the bed. "*I'll go and get the doctor.*"

"No, not yet," she rasped, her throat parched. "Water, please."

He flew over to the small shelf under the porthole and picked up a glass in his talons. He came in to land on her pillow, careful not to spill its contents. She lifted her head and he put it to her lips.

She drank slowly. She felt sick.

The image of Jamuka's empty bunk flashed into her mind. She collapsed back on to the pillow. He was gone, just like her parents.

"Jamuka," she whispered.

Fizz put the glass back on the shelf and came to lie next to her on the pillow. His eyes were glowing purple. He put his warm snout into the nape of her neck.

"*I am deeply sorry and sad he is gone.*"

"What did Ivy do to him?"

"*I checked the* Junko's *security camera feeds. He came back at 1.08am, made a cup of jasmine tea in the kitchen and—*"

"Show me now."

Fizz spread his wings. She watched the screen. Jamuka walked across the deck. It was dark, and hard to see his face, but when it switched to the kitchen galley camera she could see him clearly. He looked paler than normal, with dark smudges under his eyes. He made his tea quickly, picked up his FastPad and headed out of the door. The camera switched to the corridor. He strode along it at his normal calm pace and disappeared into his cabin. The feed cut. Fizz folded in his wings.

Now he was dead.

"*He is being prepared for transport to Mongolia.*"

She pushed herself up off the pillow. "He's gone, from here, from the *Junko*?"

Her voice was tight.

"Affirmative. He is gone. He will be buried in the Clan cave in Mongolia."

She swung her legs off the bed.

"I want to go and see him before he goes."

"We must stay until the doctor checks on you."

She stumbled dizzily over to her wardrobe, grabbed her Slider trousers and an old Smart T-shirt, and pulled them on.

"Wen called, Henry called, but I told them you were asleep. They are both very upset, and want you to call them."

"Later," she said. If she spoke to them now, it would undo her.

She turned to find the female doctor, the one who had stabbed her with the needle, standing in the doorway.

"I don't need any help from you," said Nat, grabbing on to the edge of her desk to stop the room from spinning.

The doctor strode across and took her by the arm, leading her back to the bunk. Nat tried to pull her arm away but she'd lost her strength. She flopped down.

"I'm sorry I had to sedate you but you did take out a policeman. He's sustained a cracked rib."

She cringed, remembering her chop.

"*Zoinks*, I am sorry. Will he be OK?"

A faint smile passed the doctor's lips. "He will be. He's not going to press charges. Now then, you must rest."

She took a vial of liquid out of her jacket pocket, popped off the top and handed it to her.

"Drink this. It'll help with the nausea."

Nat did as she was told. It tasted bitter.

"I want to go and see Jamuka."

The doctor checked her watch. "He is already being transported. Mr Limpet wanted me to alert him when you had woken up."

"Limpet? Why does he want to know?"

The doctor headed back towards the door.

"I'll let him explain," she said.

"Explain what exactly, Fizz?" said Nat.

Fizz pulled the duvet over Nat with his talons and sat down on her pillow again.

"*Full version of the last nine hours, or concise, factual, short, abridged one?*"

"Short one will do, because I'm guessing I'm not going to like it anyway."

Fizz put his snout up and was about to start when Ah Ping came in through the door carrying a tray. Her head was bent and she was crying softly, her tears dripping into the bowl of steaming noodles. She placed the tray on the bunk next to Nat, putting her hand on Nat's arm, and looked up at her. Ah Ping's eyes were ringed with red.

"I so sorry about Jamuka. He very good man," she sniffed.

Before Nat could reply, Ah Ping turned and fled the cabin. Fizz repositioned himself on the tray.

"*Your favourite – Singapore noodles,*" he said, sticking his snout over the edge of the bowl.

"I'm not hungry. I want to hear what happened."

"*In a nutshell, Limpet phoned your lawyer at SPIN HQ to report what had happened to Jamuka. The lawyer said that there had been an addendum made to your parents' will about guardianship if anything happened to Jamuka. As you know, before the Aunt Vera/Uncle Fergal custody battle it was they who were to become your guardians in the event of Jamuka's death. Straight after that Jamuka had it changed in the Hong Kong court to the Borjigin Clan.*"

Nat exhaled with relief. "Good."

"*But when Uncle Fergal and Aunt Vera heard the news they immediately filed a claim for guardianship stating that they are the only real family that you have left in the world. They filed it in a court here in*

EMERALD SECRET

London three hours ago. A judge has now ruled that you become a ward of court until the case has been properly reviewed."

Nat was struggling to keep up. She was feeling drowsy again. Maybe the doctor had given her another sedative.

"What's a ward of court?" she said, trying not to slur her words.

"The custody of the child, aka the ward, is handled by the court. But day-to-day care and control of the child is given to an individual. No important step can be taken in the child's life without the court's consent. The court has put Limpet in charge of you until the guardianship is decided upon."

There was an *"Oink!"* outside the door, followed by a knock.

Chapter Seventeen
BOARDING

Fizz flew across the cabin and opened the door. The pig came trotting across the rug, followed by Mr Limpet.

They stopped at the edge of Nat's bed. The pig lifted itself up on its back trotters and deposited a small package of toffee fudge next to her that it had been carrying in its mouth.

"*Sorry for your loss,*" it grunted.

Nat wasn't sure why, but that small gesture made the back of her throat tighten and tears well up and come spilling over, streaming down her cheeks.

Mr Limpet coughed, pulled the silk handkerchief from his top pocket and handed it to her.

"I know this is a very difficult time but I must speak with you, Natalie," he said.

"*I have told her about your temporary guardianship while she is a ward of court.*"

Mr Limpet looked at Fizz. Through her tears Nat could see him nodding gratefully.

"Good, good. I am very sorry about Mr Borjigin, and now there's this mess of who will be your guardian," he said. "I am here to help you in any way that I can. I hear that your aunt, uncle and cousins are preparing to fly over. The Borjigin representatives have said they first want to put Jamuka to rest in the rightful Clan way, and then they will be sending over their representative. What I need to know from you is who you want to be your guardians."

"Jamuka's Clan," she said, sniffing.

"Right you are. Secondly, I think we should put in place a block on your aunt and uncle having any access to you whatsoever until the ruling. Does that sound like a good idea?"

"Yes, and please include Prissy. I'd like to see Henry though; can he not be blocked?"

Limpet was making notes on an old-fashioned paper notepad that he'd brought in with him.

"I'll see if that can be arranged. Now then, I also have a school to run. Our only course of action moving forward is that you come to board at Boxbury until the ruling. Ah Ping will stay on this boat and caretake it. We will, of course, arrange for you to visit it during weekend exeats."

"What?" said Nat, trying to sit up. "You're saying I

have to BOARD at Boxbury?"

Her world was turning upside down, inside out, and going from bad to worse. Jamuka dead, Aunt Vera and Uncle Fergal coming to London to fight for her fortune, and now boarding at Boxbury.

She fought back the tears. "Just make sure Saskia Shiversand keeps away from me, and I never want to see her mother again."

"Understood. I will make the arrangements. We will stay here tonight, then I will arrange for Mrs Stalick, the Boxbury matron, to come here and help you get organised."

Her eyelids dropped. Mr Limpet was still talking about arrangements but she no longer heard him. She was only aware of her own breathing – the in and out of air, the oxygen keeping her body alive. Jamuka had taken his last breath. He wasn't alive any longer. She'd never be able to spar with him in kung fu again, see the pride on his face when Dragon Khan won a race, or moan about the smell of his Vietnamese weasel coffee, and a million other things, ever, ever again.

He'd been in her life ever since she was born. Her parents had chosen him to raise her. All the things he'd taught her, and was still meant to teach. Who was going to do that now? A sharp stab of pain pierced her heart.

Chapter Eighteen
URGENT MESSAGE

"What time is it?" said Nat, stirring in her bunk.

"*Four sixteen am,*" said Fizz.

She opened an eye. Outside it was still dark. For a moment she comforted herself by imagining everything that had happened was just a nightmare. She'd get up, Jamuka would be on deck meditating, Gobi would be—

"Where's Gobi?" she said, sitting up.

Fizz disconnected from his Spiderwire charge-up and swooped on to her shoulder.

"*Ah Ping put her in the galley last night and gave her extra bugs for supper.*"

Nat swung her legs off the bunk and made her way across the rug towards the door. She reeled into the corridor wall with a bump.

"*Careful!*" said Fizz, flapping his wings.

"Rats' tails, I'm not having any more medication off that doctor," she said.

She was about to walk into the galley when she

stopped, turned back and headed to Jamuka's cabin. The door stood ajar. She took a deep breath, pushed it open and flicked on the light. Someone had stripped the bed. Bare wooden slats stood on view where once there had been a mattress. Everything else was where it always was – the black lacquered frame mirror above his desk, the blown-up photograph of Dragon Khan crossing the finishing line in first position on the wall, his leather slippers on the shelf below his wardrobe. Even with the porthole wide open the cabin still smelled of the jade incense that he burned each evening.

She walked over to his desk and pulled open the top drawer. She breathed a sigh of relief when she saw that his FastPad was still there. She picked up the wafer-thin tablet and closed the drawer. She turned, averting her eyes from the empty bed, and strode quickly out of the room, closing the door behind her.

In the galley, Gobi was asleep on her perch, her head tucked under her wing, her feathers plumed out to keep warm. Nat reached over and closed the porthole. Fizz landed on Gobi's cage and mimicked her chirping. She peeped up over her wing but didn't join in. Nat noticed that her feeding tray was still full of bugs.

She unhooked the cage and grabbed a banana from the fruit bowl.

"Let's head back to my cabin. It's warmer in there."

She landed the cage on her bunk and climbed under the duvet. Fizz had stuck his snout through the bars of the cage and was blowing warm air at Gobi.

The banana didn't look appetising but Nat peeled it and made herself eat it, even though she still felt sick. She washed it down with the rest of the glass of water that sat next to her bed.

Jamuka's FastPad lay in front of her. She picked it up, running her fingers over the screen. A photo of them both in Mongolia on their horses popped up. Snow was falling, they were standing in a clearing in a pine forest, dressed in thick, long coats, curved-toe boots and big, round fur hats. Jebe, the wolf, was in the background, his black fur making him more shadow than real against the white snow. She wished she could go back in time to that very moment.

"What am I looking for?" she said.

Fizz lifted his snout. "*Your future.*"

She looked at him. "*Zoinks!* That's deep."

His eyes glowed purple. "*I learned it from* Star Wars Episode Twenty-One, 'The Beginning of the

End'. *Do you think it's appropriate that I have used it in this context?"*

She paused, asking herself why she was really doing this.

"Yes, but I need to unlock the past before I can find my future."

"That's deep too."

She began to navigate through Jamuka's messages. It was the usual load of administrative stuff that he was always dealing with. She was about to move on to his file system when a new message came pinging in, with an "urgent" sign flashing in red. She clicked on it.

From: Philippe LaPlante

To: Jamuka Borjigin

Subject: Re: **Urgent** – BlackCod

BlackCod is still in development. Max's architecture is challenging. Not ready yet for Natalie. Thought we still had three years to go to get it ready. I can maybe accelerate to get it done in two more years, before that it is a half-baked game that would be impossible for her to navigate. Sincerely, Philippe.

Sent: April 14th 11.58pm

EMERALD SECRET

To: Philippe LaPlante

From: Jamuka Borjigin

Subject: **Urgent** – BlackCod

Philippe, there have been some developments regarding the sword. What is the status of BlackCod? Regards, Jamuka.

"Do you know who this is, Fizz?" she said, holding up the FastPad.

Fizz scanned the message. His eyes flashed red while he searched the Net.

"Negative. The email address is to a blocked domain, so I don't have access to who owns it. There are eleven thousand six hundred and eighty-two people by the name of Philippe LaPlante. They mostly reference addresses based in France."

"What about BlackCod?"

His snout twitched.

"Black cod is a fish."

"Send Philippe a message from me, but copy this one in as well. Tell him what has happened – your short version, please – and that I need to speak with him as soon as possible. Got it?"

Fizz lifted a wing and saluted her.

"Aye aye, Captain."

Chapter Nineteen
ICE SKATING

Ivy pulled on her fur-trimmed warrior suit. It strained at the seams thanks to all the extra cakes she'd been eating lately. It'd been a while since she'd been down into the basement of Shiversand Towers to work out, but now, with the girl in town, there was a definite chance she'd get her hands on the right sword. She could feel it in her bones. So she needed to get into better shape to be prepared for all eventualities.

The way Natalie Walker's guardian had tried to persuade her that the sword wouldn't bestow the power and youth that she knew it would, the more certain she was that Catherine Walker had found the sword and had hidden it somewhere for her brat to find.

It'd been easy to remove the guardian from her path. He was so polite that even after their heated argument he'd taken tea with her. A lethal powder slipped quickly into the cup and bingo! A heart attack and he was gone.

EMERALD SECRET

She took the secret elevator from her armour room. When the doors opened, she stepped into a floodlit ice rink.

Alfonso, her personal trainer, was waiting for her on the edge, holding her skates.

"Saskia here yet?" she said.

He shook his head and escorted her over to a velvet-covered throne. She sat down and lifted a foot up. Alfonso knelt down and placed it inside one of her fur skating boots. He laced it up and did the same with the other. The signature drumbeat from WarZworld started to play over the speakers.

The very sound of it made her feel ready for battle.

Ivy got to her feet, balancing on the blades. The boots felt tight on the ankle. Alfonso handed her a fencing sword, a shield with the WarZworld "Z" logo on the front and a protective face guard.

"Ready, ma'am?" he said, grabbing the same equipment for himself.

"Indeed," she said, pushing past him and launching herself on to the ice.

She would never be as good as her championship-winning parents but she knew all the moves after a childhood spent on the ice.

"Couple of warm-up laps, ma'am, then let us begin."

She really was out of shape. She broke into a tsunami of sweat on the warm-up.

Once around the rink was enough. She moved into the centre where Alfonso stood waiting.

"Let's just get on with it," she said, catching her breath.

Alfonso pulled his face guard down, raising his sword and shield. She did the same. Battle time.

"*En garde!*" he said.

He waited for her to make the first move. She swiped the sword to the right and made a jab at him. He blocked it with his shield, deflecting her. She tried again, but already her arms felt like jelly.

He took his turn and lunged forward. Ivy raised her shield at the same time as trying to skate backwards, but she was so out of practice that her blades slipped away in opposite directions. Her legs were not strong enough to bring them back in. She face-planted on to the ice.

Alfonso heaved her back up on to her skates.

"Mater!"

Ivy lifted her face guard to see Saskia marching across the ice in a purple camouflage-patterned dress. She had a look of thunder on her face.

"Limpet called me into his office. He told me that

EMERALD SECRET

I am never to speak with, or go near, the Walker girl ever again. If I do, I shall be expelled. The humiliation of it, Mater!"

Ivy pursed her lips. "Did he say why?"

"He said it would be 'too distressing for Miss Walker' because our home was the last place her guardian visited prior to his death."

"I see."

"No, you don't see! Everyone at school is talking about the Walker girl and her guardian dying, and they all somehow KNOW that they both visited our house! Everyone is whispering horrid things about us. Someone said they think we actually killed him!"

Ivy sucked in her breath. That was a bit close to the bone. She'd have to find a way to scotch that rumour.

"Now now, darling, people do jump to utterly ridiculous conclusions in times of trouble. Sit tight and the gossip will soon go away. I'll call Mr Limpet and have a word."

Saskia stamped her boot on the ice.

"You don't understand, do you? It's not just me. Limpet's banned you from the school. He says if you ever set foot on Boxbury property he'll expel me. He also suggested I might want to leave anyway, in light of the situation."

Ivy narrowed her eyes and puffed up her chest. "That's my alma mater! How dare he!"

She threw her fencing sword at Alfonso and skated off the ice. She didn't bother removing her skates as she stomped off into the elevator. It was time to pay Mr Limpet a visit.

Chapter Twenty
BEAN INVADERS

Nat reread Philippe's email and climbed out of her hammock. She didn't have much time so she ran across the deck, through the hatch and down to the galley.

"You OK? I make cake," said Ah Ping, handing Nat a plate on which sat a thick slice of freshly baked plum cake. It smelled of sweet warmth, of life.

"Thanks, Ah Ping."

She grabbed a can of cherry juice from the fridge and headed down the corridor, back to her cabin. A fug of sandalwood incense hung in the air, making her cough. Ah Ping must be cleansing the boat of ghosts.

She closed her cabin door.

"Have you got the full directions?" she asked Fizz, sitting on her bunk and breaking off a piece of cake.

"*Yes. Philippe has sent them. We are to meet him at Bean Invaders café in the City. We must leave now to be there in time.*"

"Can you fetch my Slider, please? I'll meet you at the main entrance to the dock."

Fizz saluted her with his wing. *"Aye aye, Captain!"* he said, flying out of the porthole.

Nat hung a tattered old "Do Not Disturb" sign from the Peninsula Hotel in Hong Kong outside her door and locked it behind her. She didn't want Ah Ping to know she'd gone out. She set a playlist on loop through the speakers above her bunk. Ah Ping wouldn't try to get in and check on her if she could hear music playing.

The warmest jacket she possessed was the dragon waterproof that Wen had created using her 3D printer. Nat took it off the hanger and put it on, making sure it was zipped up against the London drizzle.

The rain was to her advantage. It had driven away the latest batch of tourists that had gathered at the quay to photograph the boat. She was able to easily slip out through her porthole unnoticed and run up to meet Fizz.

He was waiting at the entrance to the tunnel under the road, perched on the handlebars, keeping the Slider in hover mode. Nat crammed on her helmet and jumped up.

"Zoula!" she said, setting off at a fast clip through the tunnel.

Under Fizz's directions she zoomed up through

the City to the Slider entrance to Leadenhall Market. A valet parking attendant was on duty. She jumped down and handed her Slider over.

"Jolly fine dragon," he said as Fizz flew up from the handlebars to his perch on her shoulder.

Fizz fluttered his wings and made a short bow.

"*Thank you, kind sir.*"

"Show off," whispered Nat, heading into the market. She stopped in her tracks. "*Zoinks!* This place is ancient."

A cobbled street lit by gas lamps lay ahead. It was lined with glass- and tile-fronted shops. Each shop had a gold nameplate over it in fancy writing. A glass and iron roof arched overhead. Women were milling about in smart dresses and large hats decorated with plumes of feathers. Many of the men wore super-tall top hats wrapped with thick, brightly coloured satin ribbons.

"*I like this place. They have dragons*," said Fizz.

She looked to where his snout was pointing. On top of a gold and purple pillar stood a carved silver dragon with its wings spread.

"*Bean Invaders is the fourth shop on the right.*"

They set off towards a small sign showing an ancient Space Invader alien holding a cup of steaming coffee.

A few rows of metal chairs and tables stood outside. They were occupied with crowds of people, drinking coffee from Bean Invader cups.

"Tiger's teeth, how will we ever find LaPlante here?" she said.

"*With no visual identity of him anywhere online, it may prove bamboozling*," said Fizz.

"No one must know me," said a deep French voice behind them.

Nat jumped in surprise. She spun round to find a slight, pale man dressed in an old-fashioned green lab coat with a Bean Invaders badge stuck on the pocket. He had brown and red striped hair and thick, square glasses. If he didn't want anyone to know him then she thought he might want to lose the stripes.

"Please follow quick," he said.

He led them inside the café to a long counter stacked with cakes, muffins and cookies in jars. An industrial coffee maker was humming, buzzing and steaming alongside a giant yellow Space Invaders robot that was serving the customers. The laser firing sounds from the old game played over the speakers, while the robot hummed a sci-fi movie tune.

"*Ku!*" said Nat.

The robot heard her voice, turned, raised its mouth

into a smile and winked at her. It stopped humming, then started again with "Twinkle, twinkle, little star". The people in the queue burst out laughing.

"That's a first," said one of the customers.

But for Nat, the ghost box had sprung open. That was the nursery rhyme in an old film she had. The one where they were all on the deck of the *Junko*, her dad at the wheel, her mum holding her as they lounged in the hammock next to him. When she couldn't sleep at night, even now, that was the one she asked Fizz to replay for her again and again.

Chapter Twenty-One
BLACKCOD

"Hurry," said LaPlante, pushing on one of the mirror panels in the back wall. It swung inwards and he stepped through into a tiny brightly lit kitchen.

She wondered why LaPlante had brought her in here. He said he would be showing them some kind of laboratory but this was a kitchen with a sink, fridge, bin and a rack of shelves laden with plates, cups and napkins. A massive coffee grinder stood in the corner. Next to it stacks of coffee-bean sacks were piled high, up to the ceiling. The smell of coffee was so strong it made her feel light-headed.

The mirrored door slammed shut behind her. Now LaPlante was opening the fridge.

"I'm not hungry," she said.

"Follow me. We're going to the lab," said LaPlante, stepping inside the fridge.

Nat reached the fridge door. Her jaw dropped. "*Zoinks!*"

Fizz let out a long, low whistle. There were no

racks, no food. In their place loomed the top of a spiral staircase. Cold air gusted up its metal steps.

Nat turned back to the kitchen. Normal world. She looked back into the fridge. Other world.

"*Vite!*" shouted LaPlante, his voice echoing up from below.

"*Zoula*," she said, following him, her Slider boots clanging on the metal.

CLUNK! The fridge door slammed shut, leaving them in a dimmed half-light from the emergency footlights. Fizz's eyes lit up in torch mode.

"*I've lost my external communication connection,*" said Fizz.

"*Bon dieu*, hurry or you will set off the security motion detectors and the system will lockdown!" shouted LaPlante.

Nat jumped down the last couple of steps. Her heart was hammering in her chest.

"Fizz, fly on ahead in torch mode," she said, breaking into a run.

Fizz took off from her shoulder and took the lead. They turned a corner and entered a long blue-lit tunnel. It twisted and turned, sloping downwards, finally ending at a submarine-like open hatch.

Nat sprang off one foot at full pelt and came

hurtling through into a dimly lit underground cavern. Her boots skidded to a stop on the smooth concrete floor. A musty, damp smell made her nose twitch.

She looked around her. Rusty tool racks jam-packed with old computer equipment towered up on all sides. Cables sprang up out of the floor in snaking clumps. Wires hung down from the ceiling in spaghetti strings. Long steel tables stood stacked high with plastic boxes, and dismembered robots lay in a sagging heap to one side. An ancient virtual-reality pod hung suspended over a sunken work pit.

LaPlante had said in his message that this was meant to be some top-secret lab. *Zoinks!* It was more like a stinky junk yard.

A loud QUACK! made her jump. A big orange duck robot waddled out from underneath one of the tables. Its paintwork was dull and covered in scratches and dents. Its shiny black eyes were the old-style D2s. It had to be as old as this place was.

"*Bienvenue* to the SPLINTER LAB, secret offshoot of SPIN!" announced LaPlante, closing the hatch. "Your father started the SPIN empire here, at this very bench."

He pointed to one of the steel-topped tables. Without thinking, Nat stepped across and ran her fingers over its pitted surface. Maybe her dad had made these dents while building a robot.

"*I was here too,*" quacked the duck.

"I was your father's first employee," said LaPlante, offering her a chocolate biscuit from a tin that sat on the bench.

"What was he like?" she said, taking one.

"Very smart, smarter than me, which is hard for me to admit because my intellect is at genius level. He was addicted to coffee. Ah, *bon dieu*, your father would drink ten cups a day! We used to joke he was rocket-fuelled from all that caffeine." He threw back his head and let out a loud snort of laughter. "Those were the days."

He stopped. He frowned, his face clouding over.

"And when your father died, and your mother … a tragic loss. So very tragic. And now your guardian too. I am so sorry about that. Even now when I come into the lab, I sometimes find myself talking to your father, thinking he is still there, at this bench, next to me."

They fell silent. Nat could feel Fizz's warm snout brush her neck. Here she was, in the place where her dad had started SPIN, with a (slightly bonkers) man who had been here with him. She never knew her dad liked coffee so much, or that this place even existed.

A tear sprang up out of the well of pain that she kept such a tight lid on, and spilled down her cheek. A feathered wing-tip patted her hand.

"*We must embrace pain and burn it as fuel for our journey.*"

She looked down to find that the duck had flown up on to the bench.

"Ah, do excuse; Mangetout is both a philosopher and a poet," said LaPlante, scooping the duck up under his arm.

"Why is this place secret? Why didn't I know about it before?"

LaPlante sucked in the air between his teeth.

"What is being developed in here must be protected. There are many who want to get their hands on it."

"BlackCod?" said Nat.

He didn't answer the question but instead walked to the other side of the lab, where he pulled a dustsheet off a massive object that stood in the corner. Underneath lay an ancient, clunky Space Invaders arcade game.

"It was your father's favourite game," said LaPlante. "When he took a break from work he'd grab a coffee from the café and come back down to relax by blowing away pixel aliens on this screen. He liked the simplicity of it."

He pushed the big red button on the front of the console, but instead of the game launching on screen, the front of the machine slid to one side with a swoosh! The computer inside was gone. In its place lay another tunnel.

"Mind your head and follow me," he said, stepping inside with Mangetout waddling in after him.

"*A world of mystery awaits us,*" whispered Fizz.

Nat ducked down into the tunnel. It was narrower and shorter than the last one. There were no steps, but it sloped sharply downwards. They had to be deep underground at this point, way below the streets of London.

They reached another steel hatch, which led into a long, capsule-shaped lab.

Nat gasped. Tiger's teeth, this was the complete opposite to the other lab! It was like stepping into a spaceship. Pearl-coloured walls lit by Batalilac surround-spots curved down to a polished titanium-coated floor. In the middle of this stood a state-of-the-art virtual-reality chair that looked as if it'd been beamed back from the future.

"*Ku,*" she said with a low whistle.

"*Merci*," said LaPlante, bowing his head.

He touched the wall behind him. It slid back to reveal a silver flight suit. He took the suit off its hanger and handed it to Nat.

"You will need this to go into the game. Your father designed BlackCod for you. He architected and built the core so that only you can activate and play it. I've had to wait for technology to catch up for me to build the rest, and I'm still not anywhere close to finishing it. As I said in my email to Jamuka, BlackCod is still half-baked. I thought I would have a few more years yet to complete it."

Nat looked from the suit to the chair. "But all this stuff looks ready to go."

"It looks good, yes, but that is superficial. I had to set its physical part up to enable me to keep building the virtual world inside the game."

"Why did Dad make it only for me?"

LaPlante let out a long, deep sigh. "It is something to do with a sword that your father was obsessed with. That was all he would tell me. The game is designed so that only you would be able to find the sword if something happened to him. I had to swear on my life that I'd complete it if he died. I don't break promises so, here I am, building the operating shell around the core. BlackCod will only activate when you and Fizz enter."

Nat felt Fizz's claws dig into her shoulder. "Ouch!"

"Sorry. I have a role of importance too?"

She plucked him off her shoulder and held him in her palm. His eyes were flashing purple then green like a set of disco lights.

LaPlante sat down on the edge of the chair and let out another long sigh, like some two-hundred-year-old goat that was tired of life.

"We assume you do, little dragon, but I know no more. I have been building BlackCod for years on my own with only Mangetout to help me. It is slow work and I can't test it, because I do not have access into the core." He put his head in his hands and ran his fingers through his stripy hair. "I have lived in this lab since then. It is my life. Mangetout and me."

The duck quacked and flapped its wings.

"I want to go in and see what's in there," said Nat.

Philippe shook his head. "It is too soon. It could be dangerous because I have not built the haptic load tester yet. The challenge could overload your brain."

Nat bit down on the inside of her lip. "I'll take that risk. I've got to see if there's something in there that can help me. I'm being chased by that crazy, sword-wielding WarZworld queen who seems to know all about the sword anyway. I want to go into BlackCod now."

Chapter Twenty-Two
OCULAR INTAKE

Nat ran her fingers over the flight suit's soft fabric. It was thinner than a wonton wrapper.

"Where are all the haptic feedback sensors?" she said, unzipping it.

LaPlante looked up. "They are in the fabric, all nanothreaded in. When you put it on it will auto-mould to fit you. Mangetout and I designed and made them."

Mangetout quacked in agreement.

Nat kicked off her Slider boots, stepped into the silver suit and pulled up the zip. When it reached the top there was a clicking sound. A hood popped out and automatically raised up and over her head. The nanothreads in the fabric lit up electric blue, like veins. She felt the suit suck in, mapping and moulding itself over the contours of her body until it became a second skin.

"*Zoinks*, I feel like a robot!" she said.

She moved through a few windmill and stretch-kick

kung fu warm-up moves, testing its mobility.

"*Ku*," she said, satisfied.

Philippe waved a hand over the top of a small console desk. A holographic image of a black fish sprang up, swimming in a circle in mid-air. Part of the wall slid back to reveal a glass shelf holding a pair of silver glasses. He handed them to her.

She expected them to be heavy, but like the haptic suit they were as light as a feather. A BlackCod logo was stamped into one of the arms.

"Are these virtual-reality glasses?"

Philippe nodded. "Oui. Mangetout designed them."

She looked at the duck robot, who was perched on the console desk next to Fizz. Mangetout really didn't look like she could design anything.

"*I combined the sunglass designs of the last century with the technology of today*," she quacked.

"They're way better than the Octozebs I've got at home," said Nat.

Philippe pulled a MicroSpan tool from his pocket. He leaned in towards Nat's face. "I need to scan your right iris so that we can verify the glasses to you. Do not blink."

Nat held her eye open. A thin yellow light scanned across.

"*Bon*. All done," he said, handing them back to her. "Please take a seat."

She sat down in the VR chair.

"Welcome, Natalie Walker," the chair said, sliding back and raising the footrest to a full reclining position.

It lit up electric blue like her suit and began to mould around her, until it had completed its custom-fit cycle.

Philippe slid back a panel in the console desk and lifted out a miniature dragon-sized VR chair. It was one of the *dingest* things Nat had ever seen.

"Fizz, please come," he said, wiring it up to a cluster of Spiderwires attached to the console desk.

Fizz swooped into the seat.

"Welcome, Fizz," the chair said, shrinking down in size to fit him.

Philippe crouched down and pulled a tiny box from his pocket. Nat gasped; inside lay a mini pair of VR glasses.

"*Ku*, but can't you just wire him into the game?"

He shook his head. "No, even though he is a robot it has to come through his visual sensors."

"*I do not have an iris*," said Fizz.

"*Non*, but Max Walker gave you a unique eye pattern construction, perfectly optimised for these."

He carefully picked up the glasses and held them out. Fizz took them with his talons, his eyes glowing deep purple in delight.

"*My first pair of glasses*," he whispered, placing them over his snout.

Snap! They were on for a split second when suddenly he opened his mouth and let out a deafening, piercing screech. He rocketed up out of the chair, high into the air, red smoke streaming out of his snout. THUD! He hit the ceiling with full force. His screeching stopped. Silence.

"No!" cried Nat, hitting the auto-release button on her chair.

She leapt out and sprinted across the floor towards him. With a lightning-quick flying-kick she propelled herself up and out, catching hold of one of his wings.

"*QUACK!*"

Nat came crashing down on top of Mangetout.

"*Injured, need repair,*" said the duck, one of its wings crushed and half snapped off.

Philippe gave Nat a hand up. He prised Fizz from her grip and flicked off his glasses. In an instant the dragon whirred back to life, his eyes glowing amber.

"*Massive sensory overload removed. Normal service resumed.*"

EMERALD SECRET

"*Ai yah!* Thank goodness," said Nat, snatching him back and hugging him close.

Philippe fixed a circular diagnostic lens over his good eye and peered closely at the glasses.

"*Mais c'est bien.* We have just tested our haptic levels. I'll take it down to minimum load, which I didn't think would be good enough, but based on this test it is."

He input some information at the desk keyboard, while Nat checked on Mangetout. The duck had her head bent over her wing.

"I'm so sorry I landed on you," said Nat.

Mangetout looked up. In her beak she was holding a tiny screwdriver with which she was unscrewing the broken wing.

"*Do not worry. It is something I can repair myself. It is not the first time this has happened to me.*"

"Ready for take two?" said Philippe, handing Fizz back his glasses.

Nat's chair looked far less appealing than it had done only minutes before.

"*Lights, camera, action!*" said Fizz, flying back into his seat and putting on his glasses.

She winced as the glasses snapped on over his snout. There were no fireworks this time. Nothing.

"*Ocular intake stable*," he reported.

"Ready, Natalie?" said Philippe, handing her pair over.

She hesitated. Half of her wanted to rush headlong into BlackCod, to find this sword that had caused so much trouble already. But the other half of her was tired, nervous and grieving for Jamuka.

She took the glasses and put them on. Her skin tingled as the frames suctioned on to her head.

"*Bon.* The glasses are now tapping into your brain receptors just like normal virtual reality. Are you ready, BlackCod crew?"

Chapter Twenty-Three
THE BRIBE

Limpet looked across his desk at Ivy Shiversand. They hadn't met in person for several years, and that had suited him quite well. She'd grown vast in size during those intervening years, but more than anything she'd aged beyond recognition. Despite the Cementer sculpting she'd had done to her face, it looked like a death mask.

He was at least twenty-five years older than her, but right now, if someone came in who didn't know them, they would think him the younger of them both.

Her suit of armour and cape were giving off the musty smell of old socks. He had wanted to open the window to let in some air, but that was too risky in case someone eavesdropped on their conversation.

He'd listened to her complain about how he had treated Saskia, and how the rumour-mill in the school must be stopped. He'd listened to her rant on about the good old days when she'd been at Boxbury with Max Walker, and how they'd been such great friends.

There hadn't been a chance to get a word in. Until now. She was waiting for him to apologise.

Mr Limpet steepled his fingers together.

"Ivy, we have known each other a very long time. You didn't come to Boxbury in person to tell me all this. We could easily have had this conversation remotely, so why don't you tell me what this is really about."

She huffed.

"Very well. Let's get straight to the point. I hear the Walker girl is coming to board with you."

"That is so."

"I need you to allow one of my beetlebots to join your surveillance force."

His eyebrows shot up. "Why?"

"Because Max and his wife left her something that I want to know more about."

His jaw dropped at her blunt admission.

"I will do no such thing."

She leaned across his desk.

"Yes you will because otherwise I'll let everyone know you've been siphoning off school funds to feather your own nest."

He shifted uncomfortably in his chair.

"I don't know what you're talking about."

EMERALD SECRET

"Alpha, show."

Her vile beetlebot scuttled into the middle of Limpet's fine, leather-topped desk and flicked up its shiny brown shell. His Swiss bank account statement came up full screen. It was right up to date. He'd checked it himself earlier that morning. It contained seven million, three hundred and twenty-seven pounds.

"How did you get this?" he said, his voice strangled.

"Never you mind that, Limpet." Ivy laughed a ghastly laugh. "All you need to know is that I always get what I want."

Chapter Twenty-Four
THE ELF

Nat was inside BlackCod. She was standing in a medieval town square filled with a maze of wooden stalls. The sky above was a vivid violet. She could smell smoke and barbecued food in the warm air. People in hooded cloaks were shopping at the stalls, chatting, their voices loud and conversations buzzing.

Her body tingled and fizzed with the new sensory experience. It was a hyper-real that she'd never felt before.

Looking down, she saw she was clothed in a long green velvet gown. A pair of red jewelled slippers peeped out underneath. *Zoinks!* This was what her dad had designed for her? She looked like a fairytale princess.

She caught sight of her hands and gasped. They were neon green and patterned with electric-blue stars. She pulled up a sleeve – the same thing. She was an *alien* fairytale princess.

She wasn't alone though. A man with a blue-and-orange striped face walked by talking to a boy with yellow-and-gold zigzagged skin.

A girl came running past and elbowed Nat out of the way. She fell backwards, bumping into a wooden table piled high with books.

"*Sim lat?*" said a squeaky voice.

Nat turned to find a tiny elf in a black skirt and shawl standing on one of the book stacks, her hands on her hips.

"Sorry?" said Nat.

"Ah, you speak English. I was asking if you're interested. Interested in my books."

Nat glanced down. The table was piled high with stacks of ancient, dusty leather-bound books.

"Pick one out; it will be a cracking read," said the elf with a loud cackle.

Nat was about to reach for one when someone thrust a glass vial full of blue liquid under her nose.

"Want some dragon's blood?" said a gruff voice.

She turned. A hunched old man with warts sprouting out of his face was grinning at her and showing the only two black teeth he had left. His breath smelled worse than a dead cat.

"No, thanks," she said, recoiling.

He waved the vial again. As it moved the blood

turned from blue to red.

"It'll give you fire in your belly. Only seven shillings to you. Ow!"

"Get off my customer!" screeched the elf, her clawed fingers pulling him away. She was holding a long stick in her hand. "I'll beat you again if you don't leave right now."

The old man spat at the elf, his greasy saliva hitting her full in the face. Using her sleeve the elf smeared it away. Nat's stomach heaved.

"*Stanka quamquam stymix!*" said the elf, pointing her stick at the man.

Sparks shot out of the end of her stick and came showering down on the old man. Nat ducked out of their path. A blinding flash ripped through the air, followed by a loud farting sound.

She blinked through the smoky haze to find a pink rat standing where the old man had been. It scurried off under the table.

A round of applause broke out around them. The elf took a bow.

"Rude goblin. He got what he deserved."

She turned her attention back to Nat.

"Now then, where were we, my dear?" she said, as if nothing had happened.

EMERALD SECRET

Nat didn't fancy being turned into a rat. She grabbed the nearest book. A cloud of dust flew up, making her sneeze. On the cover was an etched title in faded gold lettering. She brushed the rest of the dust away with her sleeve and blinked. Tiger's teeth, was she seeing things? There on the cover were the words: "*The Quest of Natalie Walker*".

Her hand began to tremble. She pinched the cover between her fingers and lifted it. A musty smell wafted up as it creaked open, but instead of finding pages she found that the book was hollow. Inside lay a miniature wooden canoe and golden egg.

"You like?" said the elf, stroking the edge of the box.

Nat reached in. The elf rapped her on the knuckles with the stick.

"*Ai yah!* Why did you do that?" said Nat, snatching away her throbbing hand.

"Fifty shillings first for my merchandise before you can handle it. As you can see it's very special."

The elf was looking at her with greedy, beady eyes. Nat fumbled through the layers of her dress, searching for a pocket. Nothing.

"I don't have any money," she said.

With a flip of her stick the elf closed the book.

"No money, no deal."

"But it's got my name on it!"

The elf shrugged. Despite her tiny frame she tugged the book out of Nat's hands and landed it back on the pile.

"Fifty shillings," she said, hopping on top of it.

"But how can I get the money?"

The elf folded her arms across her chest and sat down cross-legged on the book.

"If you need it badly enough you will find it. Then come back and see me."

Zoinks, how could she get fifty shillings?

Nat turned and set off down a row of stalls piled high with vials and jars of luminous powders and liquids. Handwritten price tags were stuck to everything. Everything was for sale, so there had to be a way to somehow earn or win money. And where was Fizz? How in rats' tails would she ever recognise him?

She came out into the centre of the square, where, on a raised stage, a green-faced man was wrestling a squat, fat, hairy creature. An elf was walking around the roped edges carrying a basket.

"I'll place a bet!" shouted a woman in a hooded cloak standing next to Nat. She was waving a wad of money at the stage.

EMERALD SECRET

The elf walked over.

"Twenty says the troll wins," said the cloaked woman, throwing the money into the basket.

The green-faced man grabbed the troll and threw him to the floor where he lay, winded. There was a whoop from the crowd, but just as the green man threw his fist up in the air for victory, the troll sprang up, knocking the man clean off his feet.

Nat winced. That must have really hurt. The green man had been knocked unconscious.

The troll started to dance a fast jig. The crowd groaned. The troll threw his fist into the air.

"The winner!" said the elf, handing the troll a handful of cash.

A few people peeled away. The elf paid off the winning bets in the crowd and walked over to the cloaked woman. She reached into the basket.

"Forty back."

Nat looked longingly at the money. She needed fifty.

"Anyone want to fight the troll?" shouted the elf.

There were murmurs in the crowd. The troll started to jump up and down, beating his chest like a caveman. No one came forward. Nat pictured the wooden canoe and golden egg in the book that had her name on the front.

"I will," she said.

The elf ran over and offered her a hand on to the stage as gales of laughter and jeering broke out on all sides. People started shouting, waving wads of cash at the elf.

"Thirty on the troll to win!"

"Forty on the troll!"

"Fifty on the troll!" came the shouts.

Not one bid came in for her.

The troll moved in close, sniffing her like a dog. She clasped her nose and recoiled from his stink of stale sweat and fetid cheese. The crowd swelled and the laughing became even louder.

"A girl against a troll, ha, ha ha!"

It was hard to size him up because of all the hair. She wasn't sure if he was muscular or just plain fat. Speed was probably her only advantage.

"All bets are in. Let the fight begin!" said the elf.

Chapter Twenty-Five
THE TROLL

The troll didn't wait for Nat's first move. He put his head down like a bull and charged straight at her, barrelling along so fast that she had no time to react.

"Ouf!" she cried as he slammed her to the ground.

That hurt. Real physical pain shot through her back and legs. She'd never felt pain like it in virtual reality before.

The crowd cheered. The troll beat his chest, claiming victory. Nat had to get up. Fast. Turning on to her side she tried to jump up but her foot caught in her skirts. She fell back, hitting the stage floor with a thud.

More laughter erupted, more money exchanged hands. Nat crawled to her feet. The troll had his back to her. She took a run at him, leaping into the air, legs ready to high-kick him at his shoulder. But as she extended her legs they tangled up in her skirts. She crashed into the troll, landing on top of him.

More whooping sounds from the crowd. The troll roared underneath. He pushed off the wooden boards with his squat legs, jettisoning Nat up into the air, catapulting her out into the crowd.

"*Ai yah!*"

Hands caught her, lowering her to the ground.

"You done, are you? You've earned me some good money!" said a warty goblin, clapping her on the back.

"*She's not done; she's not even started!*"

Nat turned to find a caped golden dragon at her side.

"Fizz?" she said.

He was the same height as her. His scales were shining with a violet tint. "*We need the money. Get in there and win.*"

"I don't stand a chance."

Fizz reached down, grabbed the hem of Nat's dress and ripped it with his talons, tearing off strips, until the long dress became a mini.

"*Jamuka trained you to fight,*" he said. "*She's coming back in!*"

The crowd groaned and jeered. Nat thought of Jamuka, the fifty shillings, the book with her name on it. She climbed back on to the stage.

Now her legs were free to move like they did in the *Junko*'s dojo. She squatted down into horse stance and opened her arms out wide, adjusting her fingers into tiger-claw position. The crowd whistled.

The troll took one look at her and snorted. He pawed a foot at the ground, put his head down and charged at her again.

Nat brought her hands in towards her chest, channelling chi energy to a central point. The troll was closing in on her fast. She focused on his hairy head. Just as he was about to butt her she whipped out her right arm, slicing it through the air in a lightning-quick flash of explosive power. The energy flowed into her clawed fingers as she smacked the side of the troll's head.

He flew across the ring with a roar, hitting the ropes and then the floor. The crowd gasped.

For a moment the troll lay on his back, stunned. He blinked, grunted and got back to his feet. Steam started to blast out of his nostrils and his eyes turned red with anger.

"Throw me the cloth!" Nat shouted at Fizz.

He bunched up the strips of green velvet from her dress and threw them over the ropes. She caught them as the troll beat his chest and let out a deafening roar. Adrenalin was now pulsing through her body.

The troll put his head down and charged again. The boards of the ring were shaking under his weight as he thundered towards her. Nat let the strips drop down from her hand. If he was a bull, then she was the bullfighter.

She raised them in front of her. Just as the troll drew close she whisked them to one side. He followed the movement of the cloth and charged towards it. She sprang off one foot, popping her other leg up and around, executing a perfect flying kick straight at his head.

The crowd gasped as her slipper met his skull with a loud THWACK! The troll crashed back to the floor, making it shudder and shake.

Nat crouched down, waiting for him to get up, but he lay there unmoving, out cold. The crowd whispered words of disbelief.

"The girl is the winner!" announced the elf.

The crowd groaned and grunted in collective disappointment. They'd lost their bets. From the other side of the stage came the clacking sound of a pair of talons clapping.

"Your winnings," said the elf, handing Nat a huge pile of paper cash. "My take is thirty per cent. Come back any time."

Nat took the money. The paper was warm and sweaty. She counted it quickly – five hundred and twenty shillings. More than enough to buy the book.

"*Jamuka would have been proud*," said Fizz, helping her down from the ring.

She smiled. "He taught me well."

The troll was skulking off the stage behind her. He caught her eye and scowled at her.

"I can buy the book now. It's got my name on it. Come."

She clasped his talon in her hand.

"*I feel majestic being the same size as you*," said Fizz.

She guided him along the row of stalls, clutching the money tight in her palm. The elf was up ahead still in the same position – cross-legged on her book. Her beady eyes zoomed in on Nat.

"Aha, back again so quick? Needing that which bears your name, Natalie Walker?"

Nat pointed to the book the elf was sat on.

"That's what I'm buying," she said, counting off fifty shilling-notes from her winnings.

She held them out to the elf, but instead of taking them the elf's stick shot out, coming to rest on the top of the bundle of money.

"I've changed my mind," she said.

Chapter Twenty-Six
THE QUEST

The elf stood on tiptoe. Her eyes bulged at the sight of Nat's pile of cash.

"My price has gone up. I'll take all that you have for the book."

Nat shook her head.

"*Zoinks*, no way!"

The elf cackled.

"Then you shan't have the book."

"*You must honour your deal*," said Fizz.

The elf turned and glared at him.

"It's none of your business, dragon. This is between the girl and me."

Fizz snorted out a plume of smoke. "*That is where you are wrongly informed, elf.*"

Nat looked at the money. She might need more for her quest and it had been very hard won.

"I will pay you double what you asked for. A hundred shillings," she said, counting out the notes and stuffing the rest into the sash of her dress.

EMERALD SECRET

The elf's lip curled as she lifted her stick.

"Come closer, girl."

Her bony fingers reached out and pulled Nat in. Nat could smell her breath; a foul, rotting meat stench filtering out between yellowing, sharp teeth.

"Book for the hundred shillings plus all that money you just stuffed in your dress."

Nat tried to pull back but the elf, despite her tiny frame, had a very strong grip on her dress. They were eye to eye now. She blinked; even up close the creature seemed so real – the stinky breath, the beady eyes, the skin.

Quick as a flash Fizz's claw flew out from his cloak. He grabbed the elf around the waist and jerked her up sharply off the book, into the air. She squealed, letting go of Nat's dress.

"*Put me down, you odorous dragon!*" screamed the elf, wriggling to free herself from his vice-like grip.

"*Take the book, leave fifty shillings and scram,*" Fizz said to Nat.

"But what about y—"

"*GO! I will find you,*" he said, trying to contain the furious elf, whose face was getting redder and redder.

Nat put down the full hundred shillings, grabbed the book and ran into the crowd.

Behind her she heard an ear-splitting screech. A loud thunderclap ripped through the air. Sparks flew and flames flashed across the market.

They were followed by a loud screech.

"You'll regret this, girl! *Never mess with an elf!*"

Chapter Twenty-Seven
THE SPY

Beetlebot Alpha scuttled over to the throne and climbed on to Ivy's lap.

"*I have a spy report that I thought prudent to bring to your attention,*" it said in its raspy voice.

Ivy reached for the cup of cold Russian caravan tea next to her and took a sip.

"Go ahead, Alpha."

The beetlebot's hard shell lit up and turned into a screen the size of a small, round handbag mirror. Nat and Fizz appeared, hopping off a Slider outside Leadenhall Market. She watched them walk in across the cobbles to the Bean Invaders café. They were talking but Alpha wasn't close enough for her to be able to hear what they were saying above the din of the crowd. A man with striped hair walked over to them.

"Who's that?" she said.

"*He is anonymous, ma'am. Very well cloaked and not on record anywhere online.*"

She watched them walk into Bean Invaders, go behind the counter and disappear.

"*They went in and didn't come out again. I waited until the market gates closed.*"

"Why didn't you follow them?" Ivy said, slugging back the rest of the tea and grabbing a large slice of jam sponge.

"*The café repelled me. It has been smart-skinned against robotic surveillance techniques, just like the* Junko. *I tried several different approaches, but each time I was pinged back on to the cobbles. On the last ping I sustained damage to a wing tip and retreated.*"

Ivy's mind was racing. She had no idea who the man was, let alone why the Walker girl and her dragon had disappeared inside the café. She started to drum her fingers on the desktop, her heavy gold rings clanging together.

"Call Saskia, and get her in here. There are more pieces to this puzzle than I thought."

Chapter Twenty-Eight
MRS STALICK

Nat removed the VR glasses to find Philippe leaning over her, his forehead concertinaed with concern.

"*Bon dieu!*" he said, taking the glasses from her. "Are you OK?"

Nat blinked, assimilating back into the real world of the lab. Her mind was buzzing; her nerves were jangling. Philippe released the suit attachments from the VR chair and helped her to sit up. Every muscle in her body ached. Fizz swooped in to perch on her shoulder.

"You disappeared," she said.

"*I was ejected by that elf and couldn't get back in. What about the book?*"

"I ran to the edge of the square and opened it, but the second I lifted the cover I blacked out and found myself back here."

"Tell me all," said Philippe.

She and Fizz recounted the adventure.

"You are on a quest," said Philippe. "That must be

stage one completed. What I am concerned about is that the rest is still under construction."

She reached for the glasses that he'd placed on the desk, but he blocked her.

"I want to go back in, now!" she protested.

He shook his head. "No, you must rest, Natalie."

She didn't need rest; she wanted to find out what was going to happen next.

"You need to rehydrate, eat and sleep. Do you have any idea how long you were in there?"

Nat frowned. "I don't know. Twenty minutes?"

Philippe shook his head and showed her his watch. The digital readout glowed 6.53pm.

"That can't be right."

"*Four hours forty-one minutes and ten seconds,*" said Fizz. "*The quest has calibrated time.*"

"What? Why?"

Philippe ran his fingers through his hair, tugging on the ends.

"It must be so that the body can cope with the human energy required for the quest."

No wonder she felt stiff.

"*Mrs Stalick from Boxbury will be arriving at the* Junko *in seventeen minutes to help you pack,*" said Fizz.

EMERALD SECRET

Reality hit her like a hammer. She'd have to get back otherwise there'd be big trouble.

"*Zoula!* We'll come back tomorrow," she said, sliding off the chair and unzipping her suit.

"*Mr Limpet said you can only leave Boxbury at exeat weekends.*"

She sighed. "We'll find a way."

By the time she reached St Katharine Docks a blue Boxbury Overrider was already pulled up alongside the *Junko*'s gangplank.

"Tiger's teeth!" she said, bringing her Slider to an abrupt halting hover along the quay. She jumped down on to the cobbles. "You'll have to park it up on deck for me."

Nat sprinted to the edge of the water, took a flying leap on to the barge moored behind the *Junko*, ran across its roof and dived in through her open porthole on to her bunk.

Someone was rapping loudly on her cabin door.

"Natalie, Natalie!" called a woman's voice.

Nat ruffled her hair and messed up her bed, then hopped across the rug and opened the door. A small woman with short grey hair and wearing a blue and brown striped suit was standing with Ah Ping behind her.

"Sorry," Nat said with a yawn. "I was asleep."

"Ah, you poor thing," said the lady. "I'm Mrs Stalick from Boxbury. I've come to collect you. Have you packed everything?"

She was looking around the cabin.

"Um, no, not yet."

"Well, I'll help you then. We've got to get back to Boxbury in thirty minutes for supper. Where's your case?"

She stepped inside as Fizz came swooping in through the porthole.

"Oh my!" she screamed, clutching her chest.

Fizz landed on Nat's shoulder.

"He's my dragon robot," said Nat.

Mrs Stalick stared at him.

"I thought he was a bat. A live one at that!"

"*Many apologies, ma'am*," said Fizz, using his poshest English accent and giving a sweeping bow.

She smiled. "Very polite, I must say. Most of the robots in boarding don't do much, apart from that snake. She's about the only one with any real character like you."

"*Would you be speaking of Vesperetta?*" said Fizz, his eyes flashing purple.

She nodded. "Yes, that's it; can never remember its name."

Fizz swooped under the bunk, pulled out Nat's old grey suitcase and flipped open the lid with his talons.

"*Let's get packing,*" he said.

They were up on deck within five minutes. Nat's suitcase was bulging, mostly because of the Boxbury uniform.

"I want to take Gobi with me," she said, unhooking the cage from the mast.

Mrs Stalick sucked in her breath. "Well ... I'm not..."

"She was my guardian's. I can't leave her."

"Oh, very well then. It's against Boxbury rules to have live creatures boarding, but as long as she's well behaved I'm sure we can make an exception."

"And I need my Slider too."

Mrs Stalick held up her hand.

"That is against the rules for boarders, and there is no leeway on that one. You can ride it during exeats back here."

Nat groaned. She was off to prison.

"Righty-ho, say your goodbyes and we must go."

Nat turned to Ah Ping. "Look after it all, please. I'll see you at the weekend."

Ah Ping handed her a tin. "Cake for you."

Nat took it and gave Ah Ping a hug. "*Ku*, thank you."

"I bring you noodles in takeaway if food bad," she whispered in Nat's ear.

Those were the kindest words she'd ever said to her. Nat felt tears welling up. She bit her lip to stop them and headed for the gangplank.

The driver took her bag. Nat followed Mrs Stalick into the Overrider. As the door closed she pressed her nose up against the window, looking at the *Junko*.

Nothing would ever be the same again.

Chapter Twenty-Nine
LILIES

The boarding house was a tall townhouse attached to the main Boxbury school building. The driver unloaded her case while Mrs Stalick led Nat into a long hallway inside.

"You must Retscan here every time you go and in out of the boarding house," she explained, showing Nat the security scanner by the door.

"Dining hall and sitting room are on this floor, girls' boarding first floor, boys' boarding second floor. Access to each floor is by Retscan. Read and adhere to the rules, please, and all will be well." She started climbing the staircase. "Robots must be powered down by ten pm. Laundry is Tuesday and Friday. Prep is done in your room. Since you are in Year B you are in a three-bed dorm, sharing with Charlotte and Phoebe. Wake-up call is at seven, breakfast seven thirty, school at eight latest."

She opened the door to the girls' floor and strode in. It smelled of shampoo, nail polish and stale biscuits.

Three doors along she knocked and entered. The room was large and square with a high ceiling. A row of three desks sat against the far wall; three beds stood against another. A few posters of ballerinas and horses had been stuck on the walls. Two girls from her class were seated on one of the beds deep in conversation. They looked up.

"Say hello to Natalie, please, girls. She's had a tough time so I need you to make her feel very welcome."

Charlotte and Phoebe smiled. Their smiles looked fake to Nat. "Hello," they said in unison.

"Your bed is by the window," continued Mrs Stalick. "You can put the bird on the sill; it'll like the light, I assume. Bathroom is next door down the corridor. Now then, get settled in and I'll see you at supper in a few minutes."

She exited briskly leaving Nat stranded. The girls turned their backs to her and continued their conversation, this time in whispers. Fine, if they didn't want to talk, neither did she. She dumped her suitcase on the far bed.

"*Should we unpack?*" whispered Fizz.

"No. Let's just go down for supper."

There was a knock on the door.

EMERALD SECRET

"Delivery for Miss Walker," said a security guard, walking in.

Nat looked up to see that she was carrying an enormous bunch of lilies in a crystal vase. She set them down on the table in the middle of the room and left. Their sweet, sickly smell filled the room.

There was an envelope sticking out of the top. Nat picked it up. Someone had handwritten "*Natalie Walker*" on the front. Turning it over, she froze. "I.S." was stamped on to the back. She opened it with shaking hands and drew out a stiff white card.

Darling girl,

So desperately sad and sorry to hear the news about your guardian. I had the pleasure of briefly meeting with Mr Borjigin on the night before his passing. He was a most charming and considerate man. Both I and Saskia pass on our heartfelt condolences. Please do come for tea again tomorrow. Don't worry, I know you are now a boarder, so I have already cleared it with Mr Limpet. Saskia will be waiting for you in the carriage after school.

Be brave,
Yours, Ivy

Limpet had cleared it? He'd said she wouldn't have to see her again! Rats' tails, this was bad news.

Nat put Gobi on the windowsill and emptied some bugs from the container in her backpack into the tray.

"Yuck!"

She turned around to see Charlotte and Phoebe looking at her with disgusted sneers across their faces. Phoebe held her nose.

"That stinks," she said.

Nat raised an eyebrow. "You'd better get used to it, babe. There are plenty more where those came from."

She tossed her backpack on to her pillow and marched out of the door.

"*We're not going to win any friends if you speak to them like that,*" said Fizz.

"I don't need to win friends like those girls."

"*But Jamuka taught—*"

She opened the door on to the landing.

"Jamuka is dead, Fizz. I'm going to play by my own rules from now on."

She found the oak door with "Dining Room" painted on it and headed inside. It was like a miniature version of the main school dining room – long tables and benches with some dusty old paintings of ex-headmasters hanging from the walls. On the far table a familiar head was bent over a FastPad.

"Hey."

Zixin turned around. "Ah, welcome. I heard you were coming to join us."

Vesperetta hissed loudly and came slithering across the tables. Fizz flew down to meet her.

"I'm sorry about your guardian. That really sucks."

"Thanks," Nat said, sitting down opposite him.

"Limpet announced it this morning. Don't you have anyone else to look after you now? Is that why you've come to board?"

"There's a fight over who gets the heiress. My aunt and uncle are contesting the will so they can get my money."

Zixin's tongue flicked out. "That sucks too. And you're in a dorm with that cow Charlotte. Phoebe's sort of OK but steer clear of Charlotte."

She managed to smile. "I will. Is there a way to get out of here without being tracked by the Retscan?"

He turned, checking that no one had walked in. "Why do you want to know that?"

Nat knew that Zixin was her best, and only, option. "Can I trust you to keep a secret?"

"Who would I tell anyway?"

Chapter Thirty
ESCAPE

Nat brushed her teeth, scowled at Charlotte and Phoebe, put a blanket over Gobi's cage, climbed into bed and flicked off her bedside lamp. Fizz curled up next to her on the thin foam pillow.

Supper had been interesting – baked beans on toast. It had tasted like cardboard with tomato sauce. She'd ask Ah Ping to bring her noodles tomorrow so that she wouldn't starve.

Limpet had checked in on her during supper. When Nat complained about Ivy's invitation, he'd said that Ivy wanted to make amends and that Nat should go to tea just this once.

Then it'd been prep in the dorms for an hour, during which time she'd messaged with Wen and Henry, bringing them up to date on all the news.

Henry was about to leave for the airport with Uncle Fergal, Aunt Vera and Prissy. He said his family was a nightmare and that his mum had been out and brought a whole new wardrobe from Shan-xi.

Now Nat was in bed all she had to do was wait for the others to fall asleep…

After what seemed like forever, the whispering finally stopped and she heard the girls' breathing slow. She slid out of bed, stuffed her uniform under the duvet – making it into the shape of her body – and tiptoed into the corridor.

"*They're meeting us at the dorm door*," whispered Fizz.

There was a clicking sound and the door unlatched and opened. Zixin was standing there with Vesperetta slung around his neck like a scarf. In his hand he held a MagicEye card that contained the retinal-scan bypasser program that he'd built.

They moved downstairs, silent as ninjas, and exited the building through the kitchen back door, coming out into a side street where a GrooveCab was waiting for them. They hopped in and sped off towards the City.

"*Ku* work!" said Nat. "You could sell that retinal-scan program for a fortune!"

"Nah, I'd rather keep it for myself," said Zixin. "I like the exclusivity of it."

"Thanks for helping me."

He shrugged. "Figure you needed a friend. Besides,

I want to see what your secret lab gaff's all about."

Leadenhall was deserted. The outside chairs were stacked and chained on top of the tables. She ran up to the café door and rang the old-fashioned bell.

The yellow Space Invader bot from behind the counter activated and walked over to the door.

"We are closed," it said.

"It's Nat Walker. Philippe's expecting me."

The robot reached up and unbolted the door. As Nat passed, it began to play "Twinkle Twinkle Little Star" softly.

Nat stopped dead and looked into the bot's black shiny eyes. She felt as if they were a window into the past. Images from the films and photos of her dead parents flashed through her mind – sailing on the *Junko*, in the streets of Hong Kong, in her dad's old office at SPIN headquarters, onboard the SPIN jet, on Golden Gate Bridge. Her mind stuck on the old photo that Fizz had taken of her as a tiny baby in her mum's arms, sitting on her grandpa's terrace in San Francisco. It was her first and only trip there, back to her mum's hometown to be shown off. Her family all gone but her…

"Nat, we should get inside," said Zixin.

She tore her eyes away from the Invader bot.

"Yes, sorry."

With the door closed behind them the smell of the coffee beans was overpowering. The mirrored door behind the counter sprang open and Mangetout came waddling out.

"Greetings! But you were meant to come alone."

"This is Zixin, I trust him, so you'll have to as well."

Mangetout waddled over to him and scanned him up and down.

"No weapons. One robotic snake. Philippe says you can come in. Follow me."

They went through to the kitchen. "Your wing is fixed," said Nat. "I'm very sorry I broke it."

"Quack! Apology accepted. I am repaired and gave myself a Flaptastick upgrade. Observe."

It flew up high into the air, nearly hitting the roof.

"Tiger's teeth, that is a *ding* upgrade," said Nat as she opened the door to the fridge and stepped in.

"Wow," said Zixin. "Glad I came along for the ride."

Mangetout took them straight through the old lab, in through the Space Invader console and down into the sloping tunnel.

Zixin stared round in amazement. "My old man would get such a kick out of this. He says he knows every tunnel in London from his work on the

Underground, but I bet he doesn't know this one."

He whistled when they emerged in the BlackCod lab.

"Ah, *bonsoir*, Natalie and Fizz," said Philippe, looking up from the console desk.

He held out his hand to Zixin. "Nice to meet you, Zixin Smith. I have seen some of your work on the HackerBelt. It is most impressive."

Zixin gulped. "How do you know me?"

Philippe shrugged. "I ran a facial recognition program the moment you entered Bean Invaders. I wouldn't let just anyone in. I run HackerBelt so that I can harvest code that is useful. Yours has been, and still is, used here. Your verification cutter helped me accelerate the BlackCod development by many months. You have a genius mind, not unlike mine. You have good taste in friends, Natalie."

Zixin grinned and his tongue shot out, flicking up and down.

Philippe turned to Nat. "Now, I believe we must hurry if Natalie intends to go into BlackCod again."

Chapter Thirty-One
ERUPTION

This time the marketplace was deserted. All the stalls were gone, as were the witches and elves. Nat was standing in the centre where the ring in which she'd fought the troll had been. Now it was just a wide cobbled square, lit by two flamelamps that burned up into the night sky.

Nat stood absorbing the silence and warm air. It all felt so real. Normally virtual reality was more dreamlike than this; it had an "otherness" to it that reminded her she was only in it temporarily, for the gameplay. This was different. It was a whole new level of virtual world, more real than real.

Zoinks! Something started moving about in the book, scrabbling and scratching to get out. Keeping the cover closed, she carefully eased it out from under her arm. The scrabbling was making the book shake.

She lifted the cover a tiny bit. Long tips of claws came shooting out, followed by a gold scaly nose, pushing her hand out of the way. The cover popped open.

"*Finally I can see!*" said a miniature version of Fizz.

The golden egg was split open and lay empty in the bottom of the book.

"Did you hatch?"

He looked back inside.

"*Yes, it was very uncomfortable. I guess this is my virtual rebirth. I preferred it when I was as big as you. Why is the boat in here?*"

She shrugged. "Not a clue."

Fizz held his snout in the air.

"*It smells of sulphur.*"

Nat sniffed. There was a faint odour of bad eggs. It was like being back in Wen's granny's flat in Hong Kong.

A cracking sound, like a bullet ripping through the air, went off behind them. She jumped in fright. One of the cobbles had blown up into the night sky. Hissing steam was shooting out of the gap left in the ground.

The cobbles beneath Nat's feet began to vibrate. A deep rumbling like a waking giant was followed by more cracking and popping explosions. Cobbles were firing up into the air from all around. Steam whistled and hissed.

Nat took off, running like the wind across the square. Fizz leapt up and hooked himself around her neck. She grabbed the canoe in her hand, dropping the empty book to the ground as she ran.

"You're strangling me!" she shouted, jumping over the erupting steam vents.

"*Sorry!*" he said, loosening his grip.

She was close to the square's edge now. A high stone wall surrounded it. There was no gate or door anywhere in sight. A sudden flash of light behind her, followed by an intense blast of white-hot desert heat, brought her to a halt.

"*Ai yah!* It's a volcano!" she shouted, seeing a plume of molten lava come spewing out of the centre of the square.

It came splattering down on to the cobbles. She turned to the stone wall. There had to be some way out…

"*That corner, there's a stairwell,*" said Fizz, pointing a claw towards the far left of the square.

She took him at his word and sprinted towards it, dodging exploding cobbles and lava rain.

Another plume of lava came shooting up like a fire hose in her path. She screamed. This was too real, too terrifying. The lava started to fall and the foul sulphur smell was choking her.

She tried to dodge to her right, out of the way, but she tripped on her long skirt and fell.

But just as she was about to hit the ground, Fizz's dragon body curled and grew around her, forming a ball, wrapping her up inside, protecting her in darkness.

He rolled over and over across the square, through pools of bubbling lava. It was like being inside a tumble-dryer.

Fizz bounced down the stairwell into a brick wall, where he uncurled and released her. They were inside a tunnel. A fast-flowing river was funnelling through. Cool air raced with it. Nat took a deep breath, filling her lungs with its sweet taste.

"*Zoinks!* You saved me," she said, turning to Fizz.

But he was no longer a miniature dragon; he was a giant one now, towering over her. A sudden roar came from above ground, drowning out the rushing river.

Out of the corner of her eye Nat spied a red river of molten lava begin to pour down the stairwell.

"What do we do?" she said, leaping to her feet.

Fizz dipped a talon into the river.

"*We swim.*"

"Can dragons swim?" she shouted.

The lava was dripping off the bottom step. Fizz took hold of Nat's hand with his talon.

"*We'll soon find out!*" he shouted, pulling her towards the edge.

She glanced back. Red-hot lava versus black water. They jumped.

Nat's dress swelled with the raging river, dragging her under its surface. She could feel Fizz's claw clasped around her hand, trying to pull her upwards. The water was ice cold. She desperately needed air. What if this was where the game ended? Would she actually die?

The canoe she was clutching in her left hand began to push against her palm, forcing her fingers open. It inflated, propelling her up through the water to the surface.

Nat came bursting out, the canoe beneath her. She lay back, gulping in fresh air like a floundered fish on a Kowloon sampan deck.

Her ears were filled with the roar of the river. The canoe was bouncing along in its flow. Her clothes were soaked through and her teeth started to chatter badly.

Fizz came clambering onboard the canoe.

"Don't burst it!" she said, seeing him grip on to the edge with his talons.

The roar of the river grew deafening. She clapped her hands over her ears to block it out.

"*Exit approaching!*" shouted Fizz.

The moment the words were out the canoe went flying out of the tunnel, leaving the water behind and sailing out into a night sky for a split second, before beginning to drop like a stone.

"*Ai yahhhhhhhh!*" screamed Nat, clinging on to Fizz.

The canoe disappeared into the dark void.

Fizz unfurled his wings.

"*Climb on my back!*" he shouted.

Nat put a hand around his neck and heaved herself up. He started beating his wings furiously, slowing their descent.

"Do you think that's it? This is all there is in the game?"

Fizz flew off into the nothingness. "*There's only one way to find out.*"

Nat was drifting in and out of sleep as she lay on his back, her arms wrapped around his neck. All about was silence, but for the beating of his wings. She was wondering if they should give in and logout…

EMERALD SECRET

"*Light ahead,*" announced Fizz.

She lifted her head. In the distance she could see a faint twinkling in the darkness.

It became brighter and brighter.

"Tiger's teeth, it's a real star!" she said, seeing the perfect pointed star shape growing bigger with every wing-beat.

Fizz flew right up to it and perched on its edge. It was hollow inside. Nat climbed off him and walked into its warm centre. It was no bigger than a large doorway. She stood waiting for something to happen.

Nothing.

She suddenly became aware that they were not alone. Something came fluttering in, coming in to land next to her. She turned to find a ghostly outline with beautiful flowing hair.

Nat thought she might faint. It wasn't, it couldn't be...

"Hello, darling," said the figure. "It's Mum."

Chapter Thirty-Two
MO YE

Nothing could have prepared Nat for this. She stood transfixed, staring, lost for words. Her mum's body was all bright light; her hair flowing gold. She stepped forward and put her arms around her. Nat melted into the warmth. Peace and comfort like she hadn't known since she was a little girl came flooding back to her. She wanted this feeling to last forever.

"You made it, you clever girl," said her mum in her soft Californian accent.

She stepped back and smiled. "You are twenty-one now. How I wish I'd seen you grow up! But I know that if you are here with me now then I have died, more than likely a long time ago.

"Jamuka will have brought you up and taught you all you need to know to prepare you for what I am about to reveal to—"

"But I'm—" Nat interrupted.

Her mum carried on talking. Nat's heart sank. This was only a recording, an avatar of her mum. Of course she couldn't still be alive.

"This is the first stage of discovery for you. If you complete this task, then we will meet again."

She paused and took hold of Nat's hands.

"This is a path that will lead you to solve one of the greatest mysteries of mankind. It will lead you to the lost world of Atlantis. You will be able to finish what we were only able to start. But there are many who are searching too. You may have already encountered them. The path is fraught with danger. Trust no one. For your safety I will only give you one task at a time.

"You must recover the sword of Mo Ye. This sword is one of a pair forged in a fire that was fuelled by humankind itself.

"Mo Ye's husband was a blacksmith. His king commanded him to make him a sword on pain of death, but when the blacksmith couldn't get the fire hot enough to forge the metal, Mo Ye threw herself on the fire. She sacrificed herself out of love, saving her husband from being put to death.

"The heartbroken blacksmith forged two swords from the fire and called them Gan Jiang and Mo Ye. They are swords of love and they have been missing for centuries.

"Your father and I have found Mo Ye. It is the same

sword that was used by King Arthur at Camelot. You will need to recover it from its hiding place in Cornwall, in the Emerald Cave. Once you have it in your possession you will find a code embedded in its hilt, which will unlock the next part of BlackCod, and the quest for the sword of Gan Jiang."

She pulled Nat into a hug.

"You now have the location. Be swift and secret about it. Above all, be careful. Store the sword under the boards of our cabin. You will find a specially designed SPIN lock-safe there. Jamuka will be with you. I will be with you in spirit."

She hugged Nat more tightly and then vanished. The light faded from the star to black.

Nat blinked behind her glasses. She was back in the lab. She turned her head to find Fizz removing his glasses with his talons.

"Hey, the heiress returns," said Zixin, looking up from the console desk.

He stepped over and helped disconnect Nat's suit from the chair.

"Philippe's gone to get drinks. He's been picking my brains on some system stuff," he said, yawning. "It's doing my head in, this BlackCod. Anyway, it's a good job you're out; we've got to get back to Boxbury."

"We can't go to school! We need to go to Cornwall. I've got to find a sword hidden in a cave..."

Even as she said it, she found herself wondering if the whole thing was one big game, or some kind of joke. Fizz swooped down on to her shoulder.

"*I've checked the location and we have to access the cave by water,*" he said. At least he seemed to be convinced.

"A cave in Cornwall? Hang on, chill your jets!" said Zixin. "If we don't go back to Boxbury now, Limpet'll have the cops after us. We'll be tracked down and locked away. If it's that important we can go at the weekend, leave after school on Friday, when it's exeat."

Nat's head was so full of information about what she must do and not do that she thought it might burst.

Philippe came walking back in with two steaming hot mugs in his hands.

"What did I miss?" he said.

Chapter Thirty-Three
INTELLIGENCE

Beetlebot Alpha scuttled into Ivy's bedroom and jumped up on to the four-poster bed. He scurried across the fur bedcover and hopped on to her pillow where she was lying open-mouthed, snoring loudly.

"Baroness, I have important news," he said.

Ivy snorted, snuffled and opened an eye.

"What?"

"I have been on Boxbury night surveillance. Natalie and the Zixin Smith boy escaped the building after lights-out in the dorms and travelled across the town to the City, to Leadenhall Market, where they entered the Bean Invaders café. I waited outside for them until they exited forty-two minutes ago and returned to Boxbury undetected. They took a GrooveCab both ways. I hitched a ride there and back and succeeded in gathering certain intelligence, which is of a time-sensitive nature. They entered their dorms and are now asleep."

EMERALD SECRET

Ivy propped herself up on her pillows. "Play me your recordings."

Natalie's voice started to play faintly over Alpha's speakers. It was coming through the metal of the cab door, which Alpha had magnetised himself to. Ivy had to lean in to hear better, but it was the news she'd been waiting for! The sword! It had been found!

Ivy swung herself out of bed and went to her mirror. The tired face that looked back at her would soon be transformed to one reflecting everlasting youth. She'd become the all-powerful warrior queen she dreamed of being.

"Call Limpet and cancel my tea with the girl, Alpha. We shall prepare instead for a voyage to Cornwall. The girl and her dragon are going to lead us straight to the prize!"

Chapter Thirty-Four
HENRY

Nat crawled into her bed just before dawn. She pulled the duvet over her head and fell into a deep dreamless sleep.

"Natalie, Natalie, wake up!"

Someone was shaking her by the shoulder. She half opened her eyes to find Mrs Stalick frowning down at her.

"I thought you were never going to wake up!"

Daylight was streaming in through the window next to the bed.

"What time is it?" asked Nat.

"Midday. I decided to let you sleep in a bit, bearing in mind all that you've gone through but I was getting worried when I couldn't wake you. How are you feeling? I know how hard grief can be, taking its toll and all that. Your dragon robot told me you'd had a terrible night's sleep, tossing and turning."

Fizz winked at her from where he was perched on the end of her bed.

"Yes, I was very hot and restless."

Mrs Stalick put her hand on Nat's forehead. "You do feel a bit feverish. Stay in bed and I'll have some food sent up."

She disappeared out of the dorm.

"Zixin has gone to lessons. Vesperetta called to say he is very tired. Mrs Trogalming announced to the class that you will not be attending today due to sickness."

"Good."

There was a loud knock.

"I came to check on your welfare," said Mr Limpet, sticking his head round the door. "Mrs Stalick tells me you are sick."

Nat nodded.

"You poor thing. Just as well the baroness has cancelled your tea today. She said she had some things of a pressing nature to deal with."

Zoinks, that was a stroke of luck! thought Nat, instantly feeling much better.

Mr Limpet coughed. "Now then, if you're feeling up to it I have a visitor for you. He's been waiting in my study for the last half-hour."

She rubbed her eyes. A visitor?

"Nat!!!!"

A boy with red hair came sprinting in through the door. He flung himself on to the bed, on top of her duvet, squashing her.

"Arghh, Henry!" exclaimed Nat.

He was grinning from ear to ear. "I got them to drop me straight here from the airport. I can stay for the rest of the day as long as I'm back for tea."

She hugged him close, squeezing her eyes shut to hold back the tears.

"Ahem, I'll leave you two to get reacquainted," said Limpet, taking his leave, his pig trotting after him.

"The flight took forever. We had to travel in economy class. Mummy tried very hard to get an upgrade but they would only do it for a lot of money. Dad said no way would that be happening until the guardianship was resolved. He got really cross with Mummy saying that the trip, and our flat in London, was using up any spare cash we have. Prissy's furious because she doesn't want to come here anyway. She says it's full of Victorians and she definitely doesn't do Victorian fashion. It was a very fraught flight – well, those were the words Dad used when we got off and he had to get on a conference call for work straight away. Anyway, this is my first trip to London and I'm really happy. Here." He reached into his jacket pocket and pulled out a small box wrapped in tiger-striped fabric. "It's from Wen."

"Thanks," said Nat, undoing the orange ribbon.

She pulled off the fabric to reveal a flat box. Inside lay a jade medallion on a long gold chain. Someone had carved a girl dressed in kung fu clothes doing a flying kick into the jade. She smiled and turned it over. On the back were the words "Jade Babes Rock".

Nat fastened it around her neck. "Thanks, Henry."

"Wen said we have to call her no matter what the time. She tried to persuade her mum to let her come with me, but her mum said no, she still has to go to school, but she can come over at half-term."

"*Shall I dial her number, my lady?*" said Fizz in his posh English accent.

Henry giggled. "I want to get that accent for NutNut."

He pulled his squirrel out of his other pocket. It opened its eyes for a second, before closing them and keeling over on to the bed.

"He needs a power-up. They won't do them in economy. Prissy was furious."

Wen appeared on Fizz's screen. She was lying on her bed cutting a shirt into strips with a pair of scissors.

Nat smiled at her. "Thank you for my necklace,

Wen. I love it. It's *ding*."

Wen gave her the thumbs-up. "Got it made through a contact of Ken's. He's really sad about Jamuka. He cancelled all classes at the studio yesterday to make a pilgrimage to a shrine on Lantau to honour him."

Nat took a deep breath. Henry squeezed her hand. "*Zoinks*, that's kind."

Wen leaned into screen. "What have you been doing to your eyes?" she said. "You've got goggle shadows on them. Have you been in the BlackCod again?"

Trust Wen to notice VR goggle shadows.

"Last night."

"*Ai yah!* Tell us everything and don't spare any detail. I'm all ears."

Chapter Thirty-Five
ATLANTIS FASHION

Henry ate up all Nat's school lunch of boiled ham and cabbage.

"I can't believe you actually enjoyed that," she said, finishing the duck wrap that Ah Ping had smuggled in for her.

"It's better than Mummy's cooking. Since she came back we've had to eat from her old weekly menu recipes. It was better when she was in the clinic and Dad ordered noodles for us most nights from Shrimp Moon. Do you remember her Hawaiian Tropical Sardine Delight?"

Nat's stomach heaved at the memory. "Yes."

The dorm door opened and Charlotte stomped in, glowering over at her and Henry sitting on the bed.

"Hello!" said Henry brightly.

Charlotte said nothing. She scowled and turned away. She tossed her books on to the bed and started to rummage through the clothes in her bed box.

"She's not very nice," whispered Henry.

"Ignore her," said Nat.

Charlotte groaned, slammed down the top of her bed box and kicked it back under the bed.

"Now I'm going to get another detention," she moaned.

"Why?" asked nosy Henry.

Nat nudged him in the ribs.

"Because I've lost my games shirt, AGAIN!"

Charlotte kicked her bed box again before stomping towards the door.

"Take mine," said Nat.

Charlotte swung around. "I suppose you wouldn't miss it, would you, seeing as you've got five hundred of them!"

The words were spat out.

"Actually, I only have one of them. But you're welcome to borrow it if it will save you from detention," said Nat.

Charlotte folded her arms across her chest. "Why?"

Nat shrugged. "What do you mean why? Why not?"

Charlotte narrowed her eyes. "Limpet said to make sure you're all right. He doesn't care a fig for the rest of us. You're his special heiress. You get visitors. You get lunch served up here. I've been boarding since I was eight and I've never been allowed a BIRD in my room!"

She stomped off towards the door again. Quick as a flash, Nat leapt out of her bed and blocked the doorway. She was bubbling over with anger.

"How DARE you talk to me like that!" said Nat. "I might be an heiress but have you thought for one second that I might not want to be? I'd give anything for a normal life, with parents, in a happy family. I had a guardian who was my family and he's now DEAD. That's why I have a BIRD because it was his and now it is under my charge. Limpet is my guardian now, because there is NO ONE ELSE to look after me, while my aunt and uncle fight my guardian's clan for my custody and my fortune!"

She was shaking from head to toe. Tears pricked her eyes. She blinked them away. Charlotte was staring at her, wide-eyed. Nat stepped out of the way.

"Sorry," she said, her head bowed. She'd lost it; so un-*ku*.

Charlotte walked past, closing the door behind her. Nat found herself unable to look at Henry in case she cried.

The door opened again and Charlotte reappeared.

"If the offer's still open, please may I borrow your shirt?"

Nat pulled out her bed box and handed over her shirt.

Charlotte took it from her.

"I'm sorry too. I'm sorry your guardian died, and I do like your bird. She sings nice songs."

She turned and ran out.

Henry whistled.

"It's more dramatic here than at our flat back at Wetley Towers!"

"Hellllloooooooo!" Wen was back on Fizz's screen.

"What are you wearing?" said Nat, sitting down next to Henry.

Wen started to twirl. Her silver and aqua-blue cape fanned out as she spun faster and faster. The way she'd stitched the two fabrics together made it seem as if the whole cape was a series of ocean waves, rising and falling. She spun off camera and then there was a loud crash.

"*Ai yah!*"

Wen's rabbit robot, Fu, moved her lens across the room to where Wen lay in a heap of cape underneath her 3D printer.

"*Zoinks!* Are you all right?" said Nat.

EMERALD SECRET

Wen's head popped up. She was grinning.

"Like my Atlantis look?"

"It's *ku*!"

"I've been doing the research. You really have to find this Atlantis place. It's some ancient underwater city. No one knows exactly where it is, or what it was like, or who lived in it. How's that for a creative clean slate? I am INSPIRED!"

Wen jumped up, ran across her bedroom, cape flying, and grabbed her drawing sheet off her desk.

"LOOK!"

Nat and Henry peered close in at Fizz's screen. Wen had sketched a girl who looked like a cross between a mermaid and a ninja – spiky hair, shell-patterned kung fu trousers and bikini top.

"Will Nat have to wear that?" said Henry, scratching his head.

Wen nodded.

Nat held up her hand. "Stop! Wait! We've got to find Mo Ye, the first sword. Atlantis is the last bit. We've got to get to Cornwall this weekend."

"I'll set up NutNut to do live feed to Fu for the whole trip," said Henry.

Nat put her hand on his arm. "Hang on, how are you going to be able to come with me? Aunt Vera isn't going to allow that."

Henry pouted. "I'm coming, aren't I? You'll need me."

Nat rubbed her temples. Part of her head was still in BlackCod trying to make sense of it all. She felt the sensation again of her mother's arms around her. Could she just wire back into it, go to the star and stay there forever?

Henry was nudging her. He rested his head on her shoulder.

"Puhleeze?"

Chapter Thirty-Six
VIKING BOAT

Saskia was standing in the middle of her walk-in wardrobe. It was really an entire room specially racked out with shelves, rails and drawers for her extensive, bespoke wardrobe. She didn't like any clothes or shoes that were mass-produced, and that meant more than one of a kind.

She looked along the rail of casual dresses trying to find something that would work for their trip to Cornwall. It would involve going on a boat, so full length and corseted seemed a little too constricting for life on the high seas. Her stomach churned at the thought. She hated sailing but Mater had impressed upon her the importance of the trip and her role in it.

She held up an ankle-length tea dress with a flying-bat pattern. No, it wouldn't do. Too dull.

A niggling wave of irritation started to rise inside her. Ever since Natalie, or "the girl" as Mater had called her for years, had arrived, Saskia's life wasn't her own. She'd become Mater's accomplice and it really was most inconvenient.

The cool, refined reputation that she'd been honing for years at Boxbury lay in tatters since the girl's guardian most inconveniently died.

The sooner the sword was found the better. Mater had been obsessing about it since before Saskia was born. It was the first bedtime story she could remember her mother telling her, all about the sword that bestowed ultimate power and everlasting youth upon the one that wore the golden crown.

Frankly, she was fed up with it all. And now this stupid trip. Saskia sighed and swiped at the dress hanging nearest to her. Stupid, stupid, stupid…

"*Mater wants you to meet her in the war room,*" announced Poxo, who was sat at her side.

Saskia huffed. "She'll have to wait a moment. I have to prepare for the trip."

Perhaps she'd select a hat first. The hat would then anchor the look…

"*Mater says she needs you now.*"

Saskia groaned. "Come on then."

She pulled her dressing gown on over her corset and headed downstairs.

Her mother was standing at the fireplace, arms outstretched, while her armourer adjusted the sleeve of a shiny new golden suit of armour.

"Ah, there you are, Saskia," she said. "I need your opinion on boat hire. Alpha, show the two options once again."

A large Viking sailboat appeared on the wall screen. It had a massive square sail, a curved-up bow, a stern like a slipper and oars along both sides. A line of round shields ran around the top.

The picture changed to an interior film showing a row of robotic Vikings with horned helmets, one manning each oar.

"Regal and warrior-like, isn't it?" said Ivy. "I do like the crew."

Saskia frowned. "Can I see the other one?"

The picture changed to a huge seafaring three-masted galleon with four decks and a row of cannon poking out of the side.

"It comes with a live crew of twenty and is motorised as well as sail-powered."

"Aren't we meant to be following the *Junko* in stealth mode?" said Saskia, looking back at her.

Ivy sniffed. "I must be ready for my transformation once I have the sword. I can't be running around in some motorboat when I am the Warrior Queen!"

Chapter Thirty-Seven
THE JUNKO

Nat was sitting at the back of the classroom watching the clock tick off each second before the final Friday bell.

Professor Trogalming had put up a very difficult algebra test. The numbers and letters looked like a secret code.

Nat put her fingers on screen where the first question loomed like some unsolvable scientific formula. She felt a small kick under her desk and glanced up. Zixin wasn't looking at her but he had his wristwatch pointed in her direction. He'd synched it with his desktop and the answers to the first two questions were already blinking up in bright-green LED.

She kicked him back in thanks. The corners of his mouth twitched.

A few minutes later the bell rang. Nat was first out of her seat. Fizz flew out of the top of her locker to perch on her shoulder and they headed for the door.

"Hey, wait up!" said Zixin, running after her down the corridor.

She slowed down a fraction.

"Didn't know you could move that fast," he said.

"Mission is underway. We've got to get out before the rest of them, otherwise we'll get stuck in the traffic jam."

They Retscanned out of the main entrance. Ah Ping was standing outside Jamuka's Grooverider in the first "stop and drop" space, with the side door raised.

Nat climbed inside and took the front seat.

"Heya, Nat. We're all ready. Look. I've got Gobi, and Ah Ping's made some plum cake for the trip. Want some?" said Henry, holding out a tin from where he was squashed in next to Gobi's cage on the back seat.

"Move up, will you?" said Zixin, landing next to him.

Ah Ping climbed into the driver's seat. The door closed and the Grooverider moved off on auto-drive.

"*Drive time to Portsmouth Harbour two hours twenty-four minutes,*" announced the onboard computer.

"How was the trip?"

"Lock very difficult to do. Six river police help me.

Then bad storm last night on Channel. Big waves," said Ah Ping.

"*Junko*'s all *ku* though?" said Nat, wolfing a large slice of cake.

Ah Ping took a sip of green tea from a flask. "Yes. OK if I sleep now?"

Nat nodded. Ah Ping looked exhausted. She put down the flask and closed her eyes.

"Not much room in these posh cars, is there?" said Zixin.

He was crammed in at an angle, one arm resting on top of Gobi's cage.

"You've got more room than me," said Henry.

Zixin flicked out his tongue at him. Henry's face screwed up.

"*Zoinks!* We've got a long way to go, so be nice," said Nat, wriggling out of her Boxbury skirt and jacket. "Can you throw me my Slider shorts from my bag, please?"

Three hours later, after sitting in a traffic jam for an extra half-hour at the Hindhead tunnel, the Grooverider pulled up at the private Nelson Quay where the *Junko* was moored up. They unloaded quickly and moved out into the Channel.

Nat stood on deck at the wheel and inhaled the

salty sea air. She was barefoot, wearing her old shorts and T-shirt. Her hair was being whipped up in the westerly wind. She was back home.

Gobi started chirping from her perch in her cage, which was hanging from the mast.

Fizz swooped off Nat's shoulder on to the top of the cage and joined in. Nat grinned.

Zixin came swaying up the steps to the upper deck. He had changed out of his Boxbury uniform and put on a black T-shirt and jeans. Vesperetta slithered from around his neck to join Fizz on the cage.

"This boat's way cool. If I was an heiress I'd definitely live on this."

Nat turned from the wheel. He was grinning at her.

"You'd be an heir," she said.

"Yeah, whatevs; beats my rubbish gaff in the East End any day."

Henry came charging up the steps to join them. He stuck NutNut on Jamuka's old coffee mug shelf next to the cage. Wen was on NutNut's screen. Her hair was standing on end and she was yawning so widely that Nat could see her tonsils.

"I sent Mummy the photos of us in Portsmouth Harbour and the itinerary we're doing on the naval history tour there. She called me and said it all sounded very educational, and then she moaned that if only Prissy wasn't banned from seeing you that she could have come along too. Prissy heard her and went mad. She said she never wants to see you ever again. Mummy said that once she was your guardian then Prissy would need to change her attitude and accept you as her stepsister. Prissy went for a walk, slamming the door behind her. Mummy said she was being a typical teenager."

"*Ai yah!* Prissy this, Prissy that. I didn't get up in the middle of the night to hear about Prissy," moaned Wen. "How long is it going to take to get to this Cornwall place?"

"Eighteen hours," said Nat.

Fizz lifted his snout, his eyes flashing red.

"*HM Coastguard: Storm warning alert.*"

"*Zoinks!* That's all we need. Give full details, Fizz. This journey might take longer than we planned."

Chapter Thirty-Eight
STORMY SEAS

Saskia looked up from her sick bag. She would never, ever go sailing again. The Viking robots were pulling their oars as if there wasn't a force-ten gale and a storm raging outside, tossing and turning the longship up and down skyscraper-high waves.

She wished now that she hadn't deterred Mater from hiring the galleon instead. At least she could have hidden away in an upper-deck sitting room. It would have been way better than the bowels of this vessel.

The rain and waves were lashing the deck above. She wondered how Mater could stand being up there. And why hadn't Saskia inherited her mother's sea legs?

She put her head over the bag again and heaved at the thought. But there was nothing else left to throw up but a thin string of bile.

She loosened the ribbons of her corset and wished for the hundredth time that she hadn't chosen the blue-and-white striped full bustle dress for the trip.

"Water, Poxo," she groaned.

The poodle got up from where he had been lying next to her and trotted over to the galley at the back. The boat lurched over a wave, sending him crashing into one of the rowing robots and dislodging it from its oar.

That's all they needed, one less rower. Saskia clambered down off Mater's throne and started crawling over to the prostrate Viking.

She vowed that once they reached shore, she'd get off and take a train back home and never leave London again.

The Viking robot's arm was hanging off its shoulder by a wire. She tried to push it back into the socket but it wouldn't hold.

The main hatch slid open. Mater's leonine head appeared, upside down. Her hair and face were glistening with rain and seawater. The wind came howling in.

"It's broken!" shouted Saskia, holding up the severed arm.

"Then you row!" shouted Ivy.

"No way!"

The boat rolled to one side. Saskia grabbed on to

the oar to stop herself rolling with it.

"Row now!" roared Ivy.

Saskia did as she was told. Ivy slammed the hatch shut.

Saskia pulled on the oar. It was heavy and unwieldy. The wooden handle was rough and tore at her skin. She had never hated anyone more at this moment than Natalie Walker. This was all her fault.

Chapter Thirty-Nine
HELFORD PASSAGE

Nat and Ah Ping were the only ones left on deck when the storm clouds disappeared over the horizon. It had been a dark and terrible storm, almost as bad as the one in the middle of the Indian Ocean on their journey from Hong Kong to London.

Henry had turned green and queasy the moment the waves started to buck the *Junko*, and had headed down to Nat's cabin. Fizz reported he'd been sick ten times before finally falling asleep.

Zixin had done well. He'd made it until well after midnight, but the relentless rolling up and down waves had its effect and he had gone to lie down in the galley.

Vesperetta had remained with Nat. She'd wound herself around the ship's wheel and spent much of the night learning navigational techniques and sea shanties from Fizz.

"Jamuka taught you well," said Ah Ping, patting Nat on the back.

She smiled. How many times in the night had she imagined him standing next to her, giving her orders?

"How far to go?"

"*Helford Passage new time calculation is forty-eight minutes.*"

"Switch all systems to the MaxEdge, please. I need to shower and eat."

Nat walked into her cabin to find Henry sound asleep under the duvet. NutNut was lying next to his head, curled up on the pillow with his bushy tail covering his eyes.

She tiptoed across the rug and grabbed a fresh set of clothes. She'd shower in one of the guest cabins. On her way past Jamuka's door she hesitated and stopped. Her hand trembled as she turned the knob and opened the door.

It was exactly as she'd left it a few days ago. The bed slats lay bare; Dragon Khan was frozen in time in the photo of him crossing the finishing line. So much had happened in the intervening days that it felt like this was the past. A chapter had been closed off, and a new chapter had begun.

"Farewell," she said softly, closing the door and padding off for her shower.

* * *

"I can't look at that," said Zixin, watching Nat dig into a plate piled high with scrambled eggs.

She pushed the toast rack across the table to him.

"Have some dry toast; that always helps."

He pulled out a slice and bit into it.

"Tastes like cardboard," he said, chewing.

She laughed. "I guess you don't want any orange juice to wash it down then?"

"*Five minutes to Helford River entry, thirty-six minutes to location*," said Fizz.

Nat jumped up from the table, grabbing her plate.

"Let's head up on deck," she said.

The MaxEdge lowered the *Junko*'s sails and steered it into the mouth of the Helford River.

Grassy green hills rolled down to the water's edge on either side of the thick deep-blue ribbon of water. A light wind was carrying them in from the sea. A flock of seagulls flew overhead, scanning the deck for food.

"I wonder why they hid the sword here and not on the other coast, where Arthur's castle is?" she said.

Zixin followed her over to the rail.

"No one knows for certain where Arthur's castle was, or if it ever even existed, so maybe it's here instead. Doesn't look like a bad gaff to me for a king."

EMERALD SECRET

Nat finished up her last forkful of eggs. They were passing a small beach with a whitewashed pub on its shore. A group of people were standing on the open terrace, under a sign saying "Ferryboat Inn". They waved to them as they sailed by.

"So much for this being a stealth mission. This must be what it's like to be a celebrity," said Zixin, waving back.

Nat bit her lip. "Good point. We're going to be seen if we take this all the way to the Durmaw Creek. Fizz, get the MaxEdge to stop ten minutes out."

"*Aye aye, Captain!*" he said with a salute.

She walked across deck to the main storage locker and activated the equipment inventory picker. She located the kayaks and hit the request button. The racks ratcheted round below, the locker top sprang open, and two green kayaks popped up and slipped on to the deck.

"Stealth transport!" she said.

Chapter Forty
THRONE

Saskia lay on the deck. If an eagle swooped down now and picked her up for its supper that would be fine with her. It would be better than this.

Her dress was soaked through, her hands were raw and blistered from rowing, and her back ached so badly she wondered if she'd ever be able to get up again.

She was green too. She'd asked Poxo to photograph her face, and when he'd showed it to her, she'd screamed.

Mater on the other hand was all fired up. She'd battled the storm and vanquished it. She was a warrior queen on a mission.

A loud cheer came sounding across the water. She looked across the deck to see Mater bowing her head in a regal style and waving a hand as if she was a Roman emperor.

"Who's that?"

"Some of my subjects paying homage from their

quaint little inn."

Saskia groaned. Mater was becoming despotic.

"*The* Junko *has dropped anchor up ahead,*" reported beetlebot Alpha from his station at the stern.

Mater clapped her hands together.

"Slow up, Captain, and make sure we keep a low profile. Beta, time for you to track them."

"*Yes, Baron—*"

"Yes, *Your Majesty*, Beta, from now on. Got that?"

"*Yes, Your Majesty.*"

Beta scuttled up to the stern and jumped overboard. Saskia rolled on to her side and hauled herself up very slowly. She watched Beta beetling across the surface of the water with his paddle-flipper legs. She wished she could do the same, but she wouldn't be heading towards the *Junko*, she'd be headed to that inn, having a long bath and going to sleep for a thousand years.

"Right, let's get the throne ready, shall we?" said Mater, sliding back the main hatch and descending the ladder.

Saskia limped across the deck.

"Don't you think we should leave it and do the ceremony down there?" she said, not wanting to help.

"No. On deck. I need an on-deck coronation, not a below-deck one."

Saskia looked at the captain, who shrugged at her from the wheel.

"Oh, all right then, let's get this over with."

She stepped on to the ladder and headed back down below.

The throne was so heavy that the two of them, plus Poxo, could barely move it.

"Come on, put some oomph into it, Saskia!" said Mater, giving it a shove across the planked floor.

"It's got gold in it, Mater. We should have bought more people to help!"

"More people would have meant slower speed. That *Junko* is super-powered and as it was we could barely keep up. Come on, push!"

They got it to the hatch. Saskia tied the ropes underneath it, while Mater and Poxo climbed back up on deck. She passed the ropes up to them.

"Push from the bottom, Saskia, while we pull up. One, two, three!"

The ropes strained taut and the throne lifted off the floor. Saskia pushed up with what little strength she had left. She gritted her teeth, closed her eyes, thought about how angry she was with Natalie, and with one last shove the throne popped on to the deck with a THUD!

EMERALD SECRET

"Crown!" called Mater.

Saskia growled, grabbed her carpetbag from underneath one of the Viking robot seats and chucked it up through the hatch.

"Careful, darling. There are precious jewels in there!" snapped Mater.

Saskia couldn't have cared less.

Chapter Forty-One
THE CAVE

Nat and Henry took the double kayak, while Zixin paddled the single one. They were moving across the dark-green water at a fast clip towards the mouth of Durmaw Creek.

Thick rope-like trunks and branches twisted up out of the water at the creek's edge. The whistling wind on the river ceased. The water stilled to a glassy calm until they found themselves enveloped in an eerie silence.

A white egret came flapping out of a cluster of low-hanging branches covered in plate-like green leaves, making them all jump.

"*Stop here*," said Fizz.

Nat dug her paddle into the water, bringing the kayak to an abrupt halt. She looked across at the water's edge. A thicket of bushes and trees hung low over a white stone bank.

"Here?"

"*Yes. This is the location your mum gave.*"

"Where's the cave?" said Henry.

"It's bound to be hidden," said Nat, rowing towards the bank.

She pulled up alongside an overhanging tree. Zixin parked his kayak right up against the bank itself.

"I'll climb out and check the bank above, if you want to do the water bit. You'll be better at that than me," he said.

Nat nodded and started using her paddle to shift vegetation out of the way.

"It smells like old socks," said Henry, wrinkling his nose.

"That's all this stuff rotting in the water," Nat said, breaking a dead branch off.

The tangle of branches and vines was so thick, she wished she'd brought a saw with her.

They searched until Nat's arms were scratched and aching from pulling and weeding out the bank area. Vesperetta had helped by slithering into places that she couldn't reach, but apart from a few cracks and crannies, there was no sign of a cave.

"You know what this means?" said Zixin, joining them again and pointing below the water's surface.

Henry gulped. "Looks dark and scary in there. I bet it's full of eels and water sna—"

Nat held up her hand.

"Stop! Don't say anything else about that. When's low tide?"

"*In three minutes*," said Vesperetta.

Nat took off her lifejacket and pulled her goggles out of the pocket.

"Are you really going in?" said Henry, frowning.

"Unless you have a better idea, yes."

Zixin began to take off his lifejacket.

"No, don't. Stay here and look after Henry. I'll be fine with Fizz."

"*I can't swim!*" exclaimed Fizz.

She scooped up the little dragon.

"But you're waterproof and I need you to light the way. I'll hold on tight to you. I promise I won't let you go. Eyes on, please."

Fizz activated his torch mode. Nat stood up, took a deep breath and dived in. The water was ice-cold, even in her wetsuit. Worse still, it was dark and murky. Bits of leaves and branches hung in the water. It was like some primeval soup.

She rocketed up to the surface for air.

"Anything?" said Zixin.

"Not yet, it's a jungle."

"*Dismal*," said Fizz.

EMERALD SECRET

She dived down again. And again. And again…

"I think you should get out and we'll get scuba tanks," said Zixin when she surfaced.

"Once more, then I'll officially give up."

She took the biggest breath she could and dived down to where some old tree roots were growing out of the bank. They were thick and trunk-like. She swept Fizz's beam over the biggest one, left to right. She stopped and focused the beam on a mossy, square shape that stood out against the grey stone of the bank.

She swam up to it and brushed the moss away, revealing dark, planked wood. Nat ran her fingers across the surface until she came upon a metal handle. She pulled. It didn't move.

She put her feet up against the bank and tugged hard. Nothing.

She clenched her hand into a tiger claw, pulled back her arm, focused on the handle and punched through the water. Her clawed hand grasped the handle and she snatched it back. The handle gave way and the door opened.

Nat's lungs felt as if they were going to burst. She pushed off to the surface.

"A door!" she said between gulps of air. "There's a door!"

She didn't wait for a reply. She just breathed in and dived down again.

The doorway was just big enough to swim through. Fizz's beam arrowed into the thick, dark void ahead. Nat swam inside and pushed her way along a narrow stone tunnel.

Just when she thought she'd have to turn back, it opened out. A faint pinprick of light was hitting the water above. She kicked with her feet, up and up, until she came bursting out to the surface.

"*Ai yah!*" she cried, sucking in the metallic, salty air.

She lifted Fizz above the water and stuck him on top of her head while she trod water.

They'd come out in a cave, lit by a thin shaft of light coming through its roof.

Fizz spread his wings and shook them, spraying water in a fine mist. He moved his eyes from where they were illuminating a grey cave wall and started scanning to the right.

"Stop!" cried Nat.

A ledge – there was a ledge above the waterline! She swam over and hauled herself on to it. There was just enough room for her to lie face-down on the slate and catch her breath.

EMERALD SECRET

She closed her eyes for a moment...

"Nat, Nat, look!"

Fizz was tapping her on the head.

"Zoinks!" she gasped, pushing herself up.

Across the emerald-coloured water, in the middle of the cave, loomed a large stone. And embedded in the stone's centre was a long sword.

Nat dived into the water and swam over, clambering up koala-style until she was on top, next to the sword. It was double-edged and rusty, just like the one that Ivy had bought at auction.

"It exists!" she said. "It really exists, Fizz!"

She put out her hand and grasped the hilt. A buzz of pure energy flowed up the blade, lifting the sword cleanly free of the stone. Nat held it aloft, waiting for something else to happen, but the energy flow had stopped. She turned it over, this way and that, but it remained a rusty, ancient sword. Suddenly she started to shiver uncontrollably. She'd been in the water too long.

"We must leave now," said Fizz urgently. *"The tide is coming in fast. You will not be able to hold your breath for long enough if the water gets any higher."*

He flew across the cave to her. She gripped him in one hand, the sword in the other, and jumped.

Nat broke through the surface and gasped for air. A mist had settled over the water and the daylight was fading. Henry was huddled in one kayak, Zixin was sitting cross-legged in the other.

The second he saw her, Henry clapped his hands together, his eyes glistening with tears.

"Heya, Nat! I was so worried."

She threw Fizz into the kayak and grasped the side with her free hand.

"*Zoinks*, I'm soooooo cold," she said, her teeth chattering. "But look what I found!"

She lifted the sword out of the water, holding it up in the air.

"It's real, it exists!"

Henry whooped. Zixin reached over to give her a hand.

"Nice work, heiress. Here, let me help you with that."

"Thanks," she said, passing him the sword.

Nat turned back to the kayak and started to haul herself out with Henry's help.

"Hey!" shouted Henry.

Nat collapsed into her seat, trying to catch her breath.

"Hey!" shouted Henry again, louder this time.

EMERALD SECRET

She turned to see Zixin paddling away fast, disappearing into the mist with the sword.

"Zixin!" she shouted.

No answer. She and Henry looked at each other. She'd trusted him. Fizz had trusted Vesperetta.

"Fizz, find him, now!"

Fizz took off like an arrow. Nat and Henry began furiously paddling after him.

Chapter Forty-Two
BATTLE

Fizz swooped out of the mist to land on Nat's shoulder.

"*I've located his kayak. It's empty, but tied up to a Viking longboat. It seems that Ivy and Saskia are holding him prisoner inside.*"

"What?" she and Henry said in unison.

"*They must have followed us. Ivy has the sword and she's on her throne. Over there, two hundred metres away.*"

He was pointing his red-tipped snout into the thick fog.

"Get paddling, Henry!"

Nat dug her oar tip into the water and pulled. The kayak moved forward with Fizz lighting their way like Rudolf the red-nosed reindeer.

How did Ivy and Saskia know where to find them? What was Zixin doing? The sword, they had her sword! More than anything else, she needed the sword back. She'd have to sneak on board.

"Are—" started Henry.

"Shhhh!" Nat whispered, turning and putting her hand over his mouth. "Quiet, or they'll hear us."

The boy's eyes were as wide as saucers. He nodded and she removed her hand.

"When we get there," she explained, "you stay here while I go in. Got that?"

He nodded.

"If I'm not back in fifteen minutes, go straight back to the *Junko*. NutNut will lead you there. Got it?"

Henry nodded again. Nat turned and carried on paddling until she saw the dark shadow of the longboat looming up ahead.

She glided up alongside. Up on deck she could hear voices. Fizz landed back on her shoulder.

"*Zoula!*" she whispered.

She squeezed Henry's hand, gave him a thumbs-up and grabbed on to one of the round shields along the top rail. She pulled herself up and peeped over.

Ivy was sitting on her massive throne with her back to Nat. Saskia was standing in front of her, holding the crown up in the air, about to place it on her mother's head. Poxo was sitting to one side, next to Zixin, who had been tied up with ropes.

A bearded man was standing at the very back of the

boat, arms folded, watching.

Nat's sword was grasped in Ivy's meaty hand.

"*Boẅuẅdika rigani jowant briga*," chanted Saskia.

Zixin spat on the ground. "The sword won't help you, sad old woman," he said. "There is no sword that can make you youthful and all-powerful."

Ivy tittered.

"Oh come now, you're just bitter because you didn't get away with your little plan. I know your grandfather is desperate to get his hands on this sword. And I know that he was the one bidding against me at the auction."

Zixin spat again, this time directly at Ivy, hitting her cheek with a gob of saliva.

Ivy stood up, brandishing the sword. Nat could hear the swoosh of air as she swiped it close to Zixin's ear.

"I don't like people getting in my way," she hissed. "I should do away with you, just like I did with that girl's guardian."

Nat froze. Saskia's hand flew to her mouth. "Mater! Don't say silly things like that!"

Ivy spun around, cocking her head to one side. "Darling Saskia, how else do you think I've got ahead in life? By being a nice person? How do I afford all your finery, our lifestyle and our feasts? I get what I want through sheer force of will and cunning. I take harsh measures at times. I punish, and I take out my enemies…"

Saskia stepped back, away from her mother. Nat didn't hesitate. She came running across the deck, leapt on to the throne and executed a perfect flying kick straight at Ivy's head.

Ivy swayed but righted herself, and swung the sword in Nat's direction. Nat ducked as it sliced through the air.

She crouched down and whipped her leg out in a tiger-tail kick, wiping Ivy's legs out from underneath her. Ivy crashed like a felled tree on to the deck.

Poxo bared his teeth and was about to lunge at Nat when Saskia yelled, "Down, Poxo!"

Ivy rolled over, lashing out wildly with the sword. She staggered to her feet. Nat crouched, ready to pounce, but before she could, the bearded man came running across the deck. He launched into a butterfly kick, spinning his legs up into the air at Ivy's head, like a windmill of death.

There was a sharp CRACK! as his foot met her skull. Ivy let out a half-strangled scream and collapsed on to the deck. The sword fell from her hand. Quick as a flash Nat shot out her hand in a tiger-claw and grabbed it by the hilt, just before it landed.

Saskia let out an ear-piercing scream. Ivy's head was twisted at a right angle, her neck snapped, her eyes bulging out, unseeing. The Cementer layer had cracked across her face, revealing red, raw skin underneath.

Poxo growled and leapt at the man, his jaw wide, his *"Sharper Than The Sharpest Samurai Sword"* teeth bared. The man spun around, lightning fast, and one-inch punched Poxo in the chest. Poxo yelped and went flying across the deck, over the side, splashing into the water below.

"Poxo!" shrieked Saskia, running to the side.

"*Yavakh!*" said the man, turning to Nat.

She stood glued to the spot. He was speaking Mongolian.

"*Yavakh!*" he said with such force that she jumped back.

Nat looked across at Zixin but he was no longer there. Just a pile of rope showed where he'd been. She glanced down at Ivy's prostrate, gold-armoured body. Dead, she was quite dead.

"I deal with this. *Yavakh!*" said the man.

Nat turned and ran to the side of the boat. Her kayak

was gone! Henry, what had happened to Henry?

"*I told NutNut to take Henry to the* Junko *when we got here and fetch Ah Ping,*" said Fizz, coming in to land on her shoulder. His snout flashed red. "Junko *approaching.*"

"Where?"

He activated his torch mode. The bow of the *Junko* was cutting through the fog ahead. She'd never been so glad to see it.

Ah Ping was leaning over the front rail with a coiled rope in her hand. The *Junko* slowed. Ah Ping dropped the rope and Nat grabbed on to it. Ah Ping activated the autowind, whisking Nat up and on to the *Junko*'s deck.

"Henry in galley. I get MaxEdge full-power London?" said Ah Ping.

Nat nodded. "Fizz, help Ah Ping."

"*Aye aye, Captain,*" he said, landing on Ah Ping's shoulder.

Ah Ping gasped and froze. She turned to Fizz, her jaw dropping in shock. Fizz opened his right wing and wrapped it around her narrow shoulders.

"*Full steam ahead!*" he said.

Nat sprinted across the deck, in through the main hatch and down to the galley. She found Henry sitting wrapped in a blanket, drinking a steaming mug of hot chocolate.

"Heya, Nat. *Ku!* You got the sword back!" he said, grinning.

She sighed with relief that he hadn't seen anything that had happened. She'd have to explain it somehow … later.

"I did. Back in a minute. I've got to get changed."

Nat walked into the corridor and strode straight past her own cabin to her parents' old one that stood at the end. She opened the door and flicked on the lights.

It was kept just as it had been on the day that they died, with the blue silk blind drawn over the porthole. The bed was made up with fresh sheets every week, although no one had slept in it since.

She lifted the edge of the dragon-patterned silk rug that covered the floorboards and peeled it back. A thin brass handle was set into the middle board. She knelt down and wrapped her fingers around it. There was the clicking sound of locks opening. *"Access: Natalie Walker"* announced a digital voice.

She pulled the handle and the board lifted to reveal a long case with moulded spaces for two swords. She was about to lay the sword down in one when she remembered the secret code, which her mum had told her would be on the hilt.

"*Knock, knock. May I enter?*" said Fizz, sticking his snout round the door.

"Yes, I need you. Please can you find the code that's embedded on this hilt."

He clacked across the floor and scanned the handle. "*07734.*"

"Thank you, Fizz," said Nat. Then her hand flew to her mouth. "Zixin! We must get after him! He knows how to get into Bean Invaders and BlackCod! He knew about the sword all along. *Ai yah*, I should never have trusted him!"

Fizz's wings drooped. "*And I was charmed by Vesperetta. I hope I have redeemed myself a little though. I alerted Philippe the moment Zixin paddled off with the sword. He and Mangetout have reported back that they are evacuating the lab. There are procedures in place. He will let us know when he is in his new safe location.*"

Nat sighed with relief. "Tiger's teeth! Thank you, Fizz."

She placed the sword into one of the storage slots and closed the lid. The locks whirred into action. "*System armed,*" said the voice.

Nat got to her feet and rolled back the rug. Fizz flew up on to her shoulder and rested his snout against the side of her head.

"The bearded man, who was he?"

"*I do not know. I took an image of his face and searched. No match.*"

"Send it to the Clan in Mongolia; ask them."

Fizz's eyes flashed amber.

"*Done.*"

Nat looked over at the silver-framed photograph on her mother's dressing table. A normal family photo – Nat on her mother's knee, her father standing behind on the deck of the *Junko*. Everyone smiling. *Zoinks!* Yet nothing was as it seemed.

She took a deep breath, turned and headed for the door.

"One sword down, another to go, Fizz."